THE CLEVER STRUMPET

MERRY FARMER

THE CLEVER STRUMPET

Cover design by Erin Dameron-Hill (the miracle-worker)

ASIN: B07Q51PNK5

Paperback ISBN: 9781092852111

Click here for a complete list of other works by Merry Farmer.

If you'd like to be the first to learn about when the next books in the series come out and more, please sign up for my newsletter here: http://eepurl.com/RQ-KX

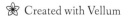 Created with Vellum

For Margaret Vickers...
...A wonderful reader and friend.
Rest in Peace.

CHAPTER 1

LONDON - LATE 1815

a change had come over the residents of Manchester Square, London in the six weeks since the Chandramukhi Diamond was stolen from the house owned by the East India Company and managed by Mr. Wakas Khan. A change, but not the sort of change Lady Caroline Pepys would have expected.

On the one hand, the dozen or so remaining students attending Miss Dobson's Finishing School had gone from living lives of aching misery and deprivation, their time spent creating frivolous handiwork to be sold for the benefit of Miss Dobson's purse, to pursuing knowledge that would be of genuine use in whatever life each student sought to pursue. Caro had gone out of her way to engage tutors in French, German, and Italian for the

1

girls, as well as dancing masters, musicians, and an old family friend who had been a professor of the Classics at Oxford and who had no qualms about teaching Philosophy, Literature, and a touch of Mathematics to young ladies of good breeding but unfortunate circumstances. In a few short weeks, the students of Miss Dobson's school had transformed from hapless penitents who had been sequestered by their parents due to bad behavior, to genuine scholars with potential for exciting future lives.

On the other hand, the house owned by the East India Company had seen a marked increase in its reputation as a house of ill-repute. Not only had a precious diamond gone completely missing from its walls, the parties and bacchanals hosted by Mr. Khan had gained a reputation for scandal and utter debauchery. Whispers of the carnal pleasures that were to be had within its exotically decorated upper rooms reached through every corner of London and beyond. Stories of utter depravity and sin abounded. Which, of course, meant that invitations to Mr. Khan's revelries were in highest demand, and barely an evening went by when Khan's rooms weren't packed to the rafters with scandalously-dressed sin-seekers and jades of all kinds.

"You'd think we were in the pleasure gardens of Kublai Khan and not the house of Wakas Khan," Caro said as Lord Rufus Herrington whisked her around the crowded dance floor in a scandalous waltz.

"I believe Wakas is a cousin to the Emperor Kublai," Rufus told her with an impish wink.

Caro laughed, nestling closer to Rufus as they swept through the close steps of the dangerous new dance. The waltz was the dance she'd been waiting her whole life for. It required partners to embrace each other as they executed the steps—unlike the quadrille or reel or any other country dance—and while debate raged throughout London as to whether the dance was socially acceptable, in Caro's mind it was decided. Because few other dances allowed one to converse so freely with one's partner in plain sight without much danger of being overheard.

"I don't see Mr. Newman tonight," she told Rufus, glancing around the room at the throng of overexcited revelers.

Men of the aristocracy blended with the newly wealthy but socially inferior. Some had their cravats untied or their waistcoats unbuttoned. One startling gentleman had removed his jacket entirely. Most of them had little care for the bulges in their breeches as they courted and flirted with the ladies in attendance. And with good reason. If the gentlemen were carelessly dressed, the ladies were barely dressed at all. More flesh was exposed to view than any Greek sculpture gallery. A good half of the ladies wore their bodices cut below their breasts and merely laughed when a passing gentleman squeezed or pinched what was on offer. A few wore gowns soaked through that clung to their form, hiding nothing. And the same outrageous beauty who attended all of Khan's revelries wearing nothing at all, save copious amounts of gold and gems, lay draped over her usual settee in the corner, garnering an inordinate amount of male attention.

Caro was dressed more sensibly, but only by inches. Her diaphanous gown revealed much, but at least her nipples were tucked under the gold lace edging of her bodice. Barely. Rufus stared at them intently as they danced, as if they would pop free at any moment. Caro should have been offended by the intensity of his attention, but she simply wasn't. She was far too enthralled by the fact that it took so little to hold Rufus completely in her sway and it had since the moment they met, quite by accident, on the night her friend and former pupil at Miss Dobson's school, Rebecca, had been rescued from her pseudo-captivity by Bow Street Runner, Mr. Nigel Kent.

"I can assure you, Mr. Newman is not hiding between my breasts," she told Rufus with a wry grin.

Rufus peeked up at her, matching her grin with one of his own. "Are you certain? I should check. It would be irresponsible of me not to check."

He whirled her to the side of the room, stepping out of the sphere of the waltzing couples, then unapologetically slid his hand into her bodice to caress her breast and play with her nipple. His eyes met hers with a challenging sparkle as he did so. Caro sucked in a breath and gazed back at him with a combination of daring and command. In the last few weeks, she'd come to view Rufus's hands on her as a delicious treat, no matter how many amorous men and women were crowded into the room with them. Most were engaged in their own wicked play instead of being interested in watching others. Although there were some, like the odious Lord Hazelton, who attended Khan's events specifically to watch others.

"One day," Rufus said, his voice low and rough. "One day soon, I'm going to do more than simply fondle these delectable orbs as a distraction while you scan the room for signs of our diamond thief."

Caro laughed low and deep in her throat, thrusting her chest toward his teasing touch. "I'm sure you are," she said in her most tempting voice, casting a glance around the ballroom. "But not today."

The difficulty with Khan's revelries becoming so popular was that a vast number of people who had nothing at all to do with the theft of the Chandramukhi Diamond now attended. It was becoming increasingly difficult to track those suspects who had been present the day that the diamond was stolen in an attempt to catch them in some sort of incriminating activity. A month had gone by since the night Caro and Rufus, along with Caro's friend, Jo, and her new husband, Lord Felix Lichfield, had bungled an attempt to catch the thieves in the middle of selling the diamond. It was clear as day to them that a certain Mr. Wallace Newman—an industrialist from the North whose factory was in danger of closing unless he infused it with cash, and soon—was somehow involved in the theft as well as Miss Dobson—who had gone missing that night and hadn't been heard from since. In addition to those two suspects, Wakas Khan's son, Saif

Khan, was clearly involved in the theft in some way as well. And while those three were the prime suspects in Caro's estimation, there could easily have been more accomplices on the loose.

"No Newman, eh?" Rufus asked, bending close to kiss Caro's shoulder and neck while rolling her nipple between his thumb and forefinger.

Caro barely swallowed a moan of pleasure before catching her breath and saying, "No. Not a trace of Miss Dobson either. But Saif is holding court with his usual coterie of admirers."

Rufus straightened, using the excuse of getting a better angle for his attentions to Caro's person to slip behind her. He slid his hand into her bodice to play with her other breast while nibbling on her ear and gazing across the room at Saif and his company. Caro took the opportunity to indulge in Rufus's attentions while he took over the work of spying.

She closed her eyes and sighed, reveling in the sweet, pulsing ache in her sex. Truth be told, she would have given up every shred of her remaining virtue—not that there was much left—to Rufus in the blink of an eye. Many were the times in the past month when she had considered taking Rufus's hand and leading him out of the ballroom—or the refreshment room or any of the numerous downstairs rooms of the East India Company's house where the public mingled—to whisk him upstairs to a private room so he could have his way with her. Imagining all the ways he might make love to her, all the ways she could offer herself to him, all the positions they could use to fuck until they were both raw and senseless, had inspired her fertile imagination to create once more.

"Have you read the latest? Mrs. Vickers has triumphed once again," a middle-aged lady with a vast amount of exposed, powdered skin said only a few feet to the side of where Caro and Rufus stood.

Caro opened her eyes and grinned like a cat.

"Yes," the middle-aged woman's wigged companion said with an excited gasp. "I do believe *The Duke's Wicked Charge* is the best book of hers yet."

"I could scarcely contain myself as I read it," the middle-aged woman said. "Every page enflamed the passions."

"Every word was like fire," the wigged woman agreed.

"My Arthur was scandalized that I could read such fictions at first, but he stopped complaining when he saw he could reap the benefits of my increased ardor."

The wigged woman laughed. "Robert was the same way with me. He objected at first, but now he buys me the first copy of each new novel Mrs. Vickers publishes."

"Half the husbands in London are lining up to buy Mrs. Vickers's confections," the middle-aged woman said. "All of London is aflame."

Caro hummed with pleasure, leaning back into Rufus and reaching behind her to cup his half-erection through his breeches. Nothing made her friskier than knowing the fruit of her pen was being enjoyed properly by those whose literary purchases were lining her pockets. How ironic that the very reason she had been thrown into the prison of Miss Dobson's school was turning into the means of her salvation and release.

Rufus gasped, then let out a rumbling breath, arching his hips into her hand. He increased the attention he was paying to her breast as well, pinching her nipple with just the right amount of pressure to send waves of pleasure to her sex.

She sucked in a breath, then sighed, "Yes, like that. More."

For a moment, Rufus followed her commands, teasing her mercilessly. He stopped when she caught her breath and let out a plaintive sigh to ask, "Good heavens, Caro, are you about to come?"

"I might," she purred. She twisted in his arms to face him, lifting to the tips of her toes to kiss him. Wicked though it made her, hearing people talk about her books excited her.

"Good God," Rufus growled when she paused their kiss to catch her breath. "If I didn't know better, I'd say you were as shameless a strumpet as the women Khan pays to attend his revels."

"What if I am?" Caro asked, one eyebrow ached, her heart pounding furiously against her ribs. "Would you cast me aside if it was revealed I'm more of a wanton than a spy or if I stopped caring about catching the diamond thief?"

Rufus stared into her eyes with intense consideration.

Caro had come to know him so well over the past few weeks. She knew him well enough to see the heat of lust mingled with a genuine longing and uncertainty in his eyes. His arms tightened around her, like a man clinging to a raft in a storm, and his lips softened as he studied her.

But instead of answering her question, he said, "Saif has barely moved from his spot, and why should he? The Duchess of Andover has her dainty little hand down his breeches while the Countess of Markham is feeding him chocolates. I seriously doubt he'll make a move regarding the diamond tonight."

A twist of disappointment curled through Caro, partially because, yet again, the evening seemed to be a waste when it came to hunting down the diamond thief, and partially because Rufus hadn't given her the answer to the question she longed to have answered.

"I haven't heard a word whispered about Miss Dobson in weeks," she sighed, taking a half step back and tracing her finger slowly over Rufus's lips. "It's as if she has disappeared entirely. And she is the only person whose identity we are certain of who has played a part in the theft."

Rufus sent her a sly grin that was half part of their act and half genuine. "There's still the thief's birthmark," he said. Weeks ago, at the very start of Caro's investigation into the theft of the diamond with her friends, Rebecca and Jo, they had determined that the diamond thief was in possession of a half-moon-shaped birthmark on his backside. "We could always start up a game that requires every gentleman in the room to drop his breeches."

Where once the idea of a room full of breeches-less men would have titillated Caro, now there was only one bum she longed to see.

"You know," she said, swaying closer and brushing her fingers through Rufus's ginger hair, "you still haven't proven to me that you aren't the thief."

"Haven't I?" He flickered one eyebrow. "Perhaps I should correct that with all due haste."

Before Caro could give him a flirty answer, he took her hand and tugged her into motion, heading for the doorway that led to the hall. Caro's heart kicked into an even faster rhythm. She had been teasing him, flirting in the way they had become so used to flirting while waiting for Newman or Miss Dobson or anyone else involved with the diamond to return to the scene of the crime. She knew she'd been playing with fire for weeks now and that the feelings that pulsed between her and Rufus were dangerous and genuine, but she hadn't expected a moment of truth to come so suddenly.

"Blast," Rufus said as they neared the crowded hall. "That lech, Hazelton, is following us."

Caro blew out a frustrated breath. "Why does the man insist on pursuing couples who want nothing to do with his proclivities?"

It further irked her that the man's very presence dampened the delicious ardor that had been pulsing through her. She still blamed the man, in part, for destroying their chance of catching the thief a month ago. According to Jo's telling, Lord Hazelton had barged in on what should have been a moment of triumph, when Mr. Newman, Miss Dobson, and Saif Khan had all entered one of the downstairs rooms at the same time. Jo had been convinced the diamond was to be sold that night, but that Lord Hazelton's untimely entrance as he pursued her and Lord Lichfield with a sordid purpose had caused the sale to be abandoned.

"Hurry," Caro urged Rufus. "Upstairs. We can lose him in the crush."

For once, the ungainly amount of party guests worked toward Caro and Rufus's advantage. They were lithe enough to dodge through flirting couples and arguing gentlemen to reach the stairs well before Lord Hazelton. They rushed up, turned the corner and darted up a second set of stairs before Lord Hazelton could mount the first few steps, then dashed into one of the secluded rooms on the second floor. Fortuitously, the room had a lock, which Rufus clicked shut as soon as they were inside.

Caro held her breath, pressing one ear to the door as Rufus did the same, facing her. They listened silently until Lord Hazelton's call of, "Hello? Rufus, old boy, I know you came this way with that delightful, blonde piece. I'll give you a guinea to let me watch you fuck her. Two guineas if she sucks my cock while you stick it to her."

Caro grimaced, feeling sick and praying the horrible

man would give up his search. His footsteps traveled to the end of the hall, then back again before descending the stairs once more.

"I don't know," Rufus said in a quiet voice, pulling away from the door and crossing the room to flop onto the oversized chaise against the far wall. "We should consider it. I could certainly use the blunt."

"What?" Caro snapped, a little too loud. She glanced to the door with a scowl before marching across the room toward him. "You wouldn't really stoop so low."

"No, I wouldn't," he answered with a good-natured sigh, patting the spot on the chaise next to him. He suddenly seemed exhausted and miserable rather than dashing and exciting. Caro sank to the chaise, and he slipped his arm around her shoulders. "Money is the root of all evil, though."

"It is," she agreed, but said no more.

She knew full well what he meant. Though he hadn't said anything outright, she understood that his family's financial situation was dire. The Herrington lands in Shropshire had experienced failure after failure in the past few years, reducing revenue to a degree that was no longer sustainable. It was the reason Rufus had been one of Nigel Kent's initial suspects in the theft of the Chandramukhi Diamond. Few families needed money more than the Herringtons. And while a part of Caro believed the Herringtons' difficulties could be solved with a change in land management techniques and a more modern approach to stewardship, she wasn't fool enough to believe that would change the expectations that had been placed on Rufus's shoulders.

He sent her a mournful, guilty look that hinted at what he was about to say, so she said it for him.

"Your father is demanding you marry well and quickly, isn't he?"

Rufus stared at her for a moment with a stricken look, then blew out a breath and ran a hand through his fiery hair. "He's all but arranged a marriage to Lady Malvis Cunningham."

"Lady Malvis?"

Caro nearly laughed in spite of Rufus's depressed spirits. Lady Malvis Cunningham had been engaged to Jo's new husband, Lord Felix Lichfield, months ago, but had called off the engagement when she discovered Felix's reputation for bedsport that the Marquis deSade would be proud of. Little did Lady Malvis know that Felix's reputation had been unwanted and that he had thoroughly changed his ways upon his marriage to Jo. It was a delicious sort of irony that she should have set her marital sights on Felix's closest friend now.

Evidently, Caro wasn't able to hide her mirth well enough. Rufus sent her a sullen look. "Please don't laugh at my misfortune."

"I'm not laughing, darling," she said, scooting closer to him and cradling his face, though she couldn't wipe the smile from her own. "I know how you feel about this."

"Do you?" he asked, raising an eyebrow. "Do you know that I only come here to assist you in your search for the diamond thief because it allows me to misbehave scandalously with you?"

"That's not true," Caro told him gently. "You're as concerned about the thief as I am."

"Am I?" He whisked her into his arms, twisting to lie her on her back under him. He managed to slip her gown off her shoulders and tug it just enough so that both breasts popped free of the silken fabric. He cupped one hand around a breast, kneading it gently. "Do you know how desperately I long to make you mine, how badly I want to sink my cock deep into your quivering pussy until we both come so hard we black out?"

Caro caught her breath, brushing her hands up his sides and resting them on his shoulders. "Yes, I do," she said earnestly. "You want it as madly as I do. I don't understand why you haven't claimed what you want already."

His eyebrows lifted as he stared at her. "Because you're not one of Khan's cheap whores," he said. "You're Lady Caroline Pepys. You hail from a distinguished family. Your father is an earl."

"That doesn't mean I don't get wet when you fiddle with me the way you are," Caro said, torn between wanting to laugh at the paradoxical sweetness of the way he seemed to see her and wanting to tear open his breeches and force the matter there and then by riding him until his eyes rolled back in his head with pleasure.

His body tensed, and for a brief moment she was certain he would burrow under her skirts to see if what she said was true. All too soon, he shook his head and sat straight.

"I'm going to have to marry Lady Malvis." He said her name as though tasting a particularly salty fish. "But I don't want to give you up," he added. Caro sat up, doing nothing to adjust her bodice or hide the full expanse of her breasts from him as he rushed on with, "I can't marry you, but say you'll be my mistress. I'll keep you in grand style. You'll want for nothing. As soon as I do my duty by Lady Malvis, I'll put her off and devote myself exclusively to you, to the family we could have together."

Caro's heart flopped in her chest, and she sent him a sad smile. "You know you don't have the money for any of that," she said softly.

"Lady Malvis brings quite a price with her," he argued.

"A price which would go to your father and your family's estate," she pointed out.

"Yes, but...." He clenched his jaw, and when no words came out, he blew out a defeated sigh and scrubbed his hands over his face. "It's over, then," he said, shoulders dropping. "I am utterly at the mercy of a title I never asked for and a family I am a part of completely by accident. Would that I were a pauper who could claim his own life and the woman he loves." He glanced meaningfully at Caro.

Flutters of bitter sweetness swirled through Caro's insides and her soul. Rufus loved her. She'd suspected as much for weeks. It had come upon them both suddenly and furiously as they'd set every rule of propriety aside to engage in their wicked flirtations while trying to catch the diamond thief. And if Rufus's situation were the only one in play, theirs would have been a tragic love indeed. But there were a great many things about her that Rufus didn't yet know. Things that might turn the tide when they became known.

"We need to focus on what truly matters at the moment," she said, inching closer to him. She reached for his hand and lifted it to cradle one of her exposed breasts. "We need to return to the ballroom where we can flirt and tease and pretend to be as careless as any other of Khan's guests, all the while keeping our eyes peeled for the diamond thief and his accomplices."

"But what if we catch the thief?" Rufus asked. "What if Newman or Miss Dobson returns and we nab them and the game is up? What of us then?"

A slow, clever grin spread across Caro's face. There was so much that Rufus had yet to learn, so much that would change everything. "Why don't you leave the future to me?" she asked. "I have plans for it, after all."

"And do those plans involve me?" Rufus asked, kneading her breast and rubbing his palm across her nipple to make it hard once more.

"Of course they do," Caro answered, mischief in her eyes.

CHAPTER 2

*P*lots and schemes to alleviate the unfortunate situation Rufus found himself in reverberated through Caro's brain all through the night and into the next morning. Of course, she knew the course of action she planned to take. Indeed, she'd been hard at work doing everything she could to provide just the sort of windfall Rufus and the entire Herrington family would need to change not only their fortunes, but their way of thinking. The way her pen scratched across the paper in front of her was proof of that. Her hand was beginning to cramp, seeing as she had been writing since dawn in the office once occupied by Miss Dobson. But as she'd hoped, her publisher had sent her a note just that morning begging for more material. He could hardly produce Mrs. Vickers books fast enough to meet the voracious demands of the readers.

"She brushed her lips softly against his," she wrote,

"her heart aching for the losses he had experienced, but if she had her way, other parts of her would be aching in no time as she allowed him to have his wicked way with her.

"'Is this what you want, my lord?' she asked, stepping back and letting the robe slip from her shoulders to reveal her fresh, virginal skin and the gossamer curls between her legs.

"'Yes,' Lord Darkington told her. 'I want it all. I want you on your knees.'

"Felicia lowered her eyes and did as she was commanded.

"'Now, unleash my dragon and give him a home in the sweet cave of your mouth.'"

A knock sounded at the office door, jolting Caro out of her overheated imagination so sharply that ink splattered across the page.

"Lady Caroline, Lady Caroline," Flora, the school's loyal, if flighty, maid burst into the room. Her brown eyes were wide and her uniform cap was askew. "You're needed immediately."

Caro reached for a scrap of blotting paper and touched it discretely to the wet ink before standing. "What seems to be the trouble?" she asked, loath to step away from her desk.

"It's Lady Alphonse and Lady Towers," Flora said. "They've come to demand a reckoning."

Caro's brow shot up. She should have grown used to the parents of the few remaining students pestering her with their concerns and inquiries, but each new visit to the school and the demands they brought with them irritated her. She had things perfectly well in hand, after all.

"Tell them I'll be there—no, I'll tell them myself."

She stepped away from the desk, sending a last, lingering glance of worry at her manuscript. Felicity and Eliza would be in the room within seconds to pore over what she'd already written. Caro didn't know whether to love them for their wickedness or to be exasperated for their nosiness.

As soon as she reached the hall, the new sounds of the school swelled in chorus around her. In the room across the hall from her office, three of the girls were in the midst of a music lesson, one of them playing while the other two sang a duet. Farther down the hall, the voice of Dr. Brunning as he lectured half a dozen young ladies about Socratic method sounded through the door to one of the classrooms. Closer to the front of the hall, a trio of pupils were arguing fiercely about something in German. And standing near the front door were Lady Alphonse and Lady Towers.

"Good morning, my ladies." As she reached the two, startled women, Caro dropped into a perfect curtsy. "May I be of some assistance this morning?"

Lady Alphonse blinked rapidly and shook her head as though she were attempting to wake herself from a dream. "Now see here, young lady," she began, though perhaps without the force those words should have carried. "I am entirely displeased with the fact that you have continued operation of this institution without its founder."

With as pleasant an expression as Caro could manage at any mention of the horrible Miss Dobson, she said, "Miss Dobson abandoned the school and has not been heard from since. However, we, the pupils of this school, decided that our intellectual and moral education was of paramount importance and that the school should remain open for our benefit."

She wanted to grin like a cat over the baffled expressions her explanation prompted in the two grand ladies in front of her. The explanation had been crafted and refined after similar visits from anxious parents intent on taking their daughters home. Caro refused to simply bow to pressure, however, and since she was rather too old to continue on as a pupil herself at the ripe age of three-and-twenty, she had declared herself the new mistress of the establishment.

"But," Lady Towers stammered, exactly as Caro expected. "But you cannot simply turn a school over to its students. Where is the order of it all? Where is the hierarchy?"

In answer to her question, Caro followed the script she had perfected and gestured for the ladies to follow her down the hall as though giving a tour.

"As you can see, we have engaged educators of the finest renown to take Miss Dobson's place." She crossed to one of the classrooms and opened the door to reveal four young ladies sitting at a table, slates ready, while a stolid man of the cloth lectured them about the Gospels. "Rev. Ellis has taken over the spiritual guidance of our students," Caro explained in a quiet voice.

"Oh, hello." Rev. Ellis interrupted his lesson to nod gravely to the two, fine ladies. "Would you care to attend to the lessons of the life of our Lord Jesus?"

"Oh, no, no, carry on," Lady Alphonse said, backing away from the room as though she had interrupted a vicar in the middle of his sermon. Once Caro had shut the door, she said, "I don't recall Miss Dobson having a man of the cloth on staff to instruct the young ladies," in a respectful voice.

"She didn't," Caro said, leading them on toward the dining room. "But it was an oversight we sought to correct immediately upon her disappearance."

She didn't need to elaborate in order to inform the two ladies that the purpose of the new spiritual lessons were to equip the young ladies with the ability to question what they learned in church from a rational viewpoint as well as to learn the true words of the Bible rather than simply what they were told.

They turned the corner into the dining room, where two of the remaining pupils were listening to Mrs. Murphy, the school's new cook, explain proper table settings and meal management.

"I cannot stress enough the importance of frugality without sacrificing quality," Mrs. Murphy told the young ladies with a shake of her finger. "When you are running your own households, you'll thank me."

"Yes, ma'am," the two young ladies said earnestly.

"I don't recall Miss Dobson teaching the skills our girls will need in their married lives," Lady Towers said, her expression brightening. "In fact, I'd given up all hope of my Eliza ever making a suitable wife, but now...."

"That is the reason your daughters were sent to this school, is it not? To erase their past transgressions and prepare them for a new, respectable life?" Caro questioned both women, trying not to give in to her temper. In fact, she knew full well most of her friends and fellow pupils had been sent to the school to be forgotten as hopeless.

"Oh, yes," Lady Towers said with sudden seriousness, her cheeks glowing pink.

"Absolutely," Lady Alphonse agreed. "Didn't I say our girls would be washed as clean as the morning dew and ready to rejoin polite society after their time here?"

"You always did." Lady Towers nodded.

Caro clenched her jaw, but tried to smile all the same. If she had her druthers, her friends would learn what they needed to hold their own against their callous, unfeeling families. They might not be able to break free of the rigid social lines that would hold them in place for the rest of their lives, but they would have imagination, knowledge, and a liberal education in all the ways that a woman could secretly enjoy herself and her life by the time they returned to the world.

"As you can see," she lectured the two fine ladies as

she led their tour toward the music room, "we have adjusted to Miss Dobson's absence and are thriving."

"Yes, I can see you are," Lady Towers said, smiling as the strains of a Handel aria wafted down the hall. "I told you there was nothing to fear," she said to Lady Alphonse.

"I believe it was *I* who told *you* things were well in hand," Lady Alphonse argued.

Caro managed to keep her brittle smile in place by marveling at how easily the two had been swayed. It had taken other mothers—and an occasional father—far longer to come around to Caro's way of thinking. But she'd won her way in the end every time.

She was about to open her mouth to invite the two women for tea in one of the unused classrooms that she'd had redecorated specifically for the purpose of wooing hesitant parents, when Lady Towers said, "Miss Dobson will be in quite a pickle when she returns from her father's country house."

Caro's mouth dropped open and her pulse sped up.

"I dare say she will," Lady Alphonse said. "But I do have one further concern." She turned to Caro, her expression growing serious once more. "How do you respond to the unfortunate reputation of the house next door?"

Caro could have screamed. Not so much as a trace of Miss Dobson for weeks, and the moment the answer to the mystery of the woman's whereabouts had been dropped in her lap, the subject had been changed to the stickiest topic of all.

"We have very little interaction with our neighbors," she told the women, frustrated as she felt her face grow hot. Blushing was a terrible accompaniment to lies.

"But the influence," Lady Towers said. "I cannot help but worry that my poor, innocent, impressionable Eliza might glance out the window at an inopportune time and see examples of lust and depravity." She lowered her voice to a whisper at her last words.

Caro resisted the urge to arch an incredulous brow. The only reason Eliza and Felicity hadn't become embroiled in the entertainments on offer at the East India Company's house was because they did not yet know about the secret passageways. But if the two ever found out, Caro was certain they would be dancing naked in the ballroom on a nightly basis.

"I can assure you—" she began, but was sharply cut short.

"Caroline!"

Cold fingers of dread slipped down Caro's spine, snapping her posture rod straight. She turned to glance toward the front of the hallway only to find her own mother standing inside the front door like a framed portrait of a Valkyrie about to pass judgment.

"If you will excuse me for a moment," Caro whispered to Lady Alphonse and Lady Towers. "Please feel free to observe the music class, if you'd like."

She steered the two women—who seemed as alarmed

by her mother's appearance as Caro was—toward the music room. Once they were on their way, she squared her shoulders, tilted her head up, and marched down the hall toward her mother.

"What a pleasant surprise, Mother," she said with the best smile she could manage, which was as sour as if she'd just sucked on a lemon. "What brings you to our humble school this morning?"

"Miss Dobson's school, you mean," her mother snapped, looking this way and that. "Where is the old prune?"

Caro lost her smile and tried not to lose her confidence with it. "Surely, you've heard, Mama. Miss Dobson has abandoned the school."

Her mother blinked, staring hard at Caro. "How? When?"

Caro cleared her throat, her stomach sinking. "More than a month ago. Do you not remember?"

"No," her mother said with a frown.

Caro hesitated for only a moment before saying, "I sent you a letter." Indeed, she had. One that informed her mother not only of Miss Dobson's disappearance, but of her intention to take the school in hand.

Her mother waved her hand as though swatting a fly. "You know I never read your horrid drivel."

Caro swallowed hard. There it was—the reason her mother had shunted her off to a fourth-rate reformatory and left her there to rot. Her writing. She cleared her throat and did her very best to scrape up her pride enough to say, "Miss Dobson is gone, and we, her students, have decided to carry on under new management."

"What do I care?" her mother said, hissing impatiently. "This place could be managed by a rag-picker, for all I am concerned. For all you are concerned as well."

"I—" Caro opened her mouth to defend her decisions and to argue all the reasons that her mother should, indeed, care, but she came up short at the tail end of her mother's statement. "I most certainly do care about the quality of education and attention offered at the institution I am such an integral part of."

"You won't be part of it for long," her mother said with a sigh. "Now fetch your bonnet and come along."

"I will not." Caro regretted how much like a disobedient child she sounded. Even more so when her mother glared at her with a ferocity that made even Caro's stalwart heart quiver. "That is," she corrected herself, voice hoarse, "I require an explanation before I abandon my work here."

"You require nothing," her mother boomed. "You will do as you are told." She paused, then clicked her tongue impatiently. "Very well, if it will stop you from being so stubborn."

Something about the way her mother made the comment forced Caro to realize she'd crossed her arms tightly and was facing her mother with the same insolent look she'd worn as a girl of fifteen being forced to hold her tongue at family gatherings. She let her arms drop and assumed a more dignified, mature posture. Unfortunately, that brought a pleased smile to her mother's face, which Caro loathed.

"You are to be married," her mother said a moment later, wiping all expression from Caro's face.

"Married?" Her stomach twisted and her thoughts flew instantly to Rufus. It was one thing to think of him forced to engage himself to another woman—something she was still determined would never happen—but it was quite another to find herself in the line of fire.

"Yes," her mother said with a sniff. "And to the heir to an earldom as well."

Caro's brow flew up. Her mother had thought enough of her to engage her to the heir to an earldom? Surely that was the sort of honor that should have gone to her perfect, glorious, well-behaved, younger sister, Georgiana. Georgiana could do no wrong. Georgiana was the darling, perfect daughter. Georgiana was the one who had let slip to her mother that Caro was none other than the notorious authoress, Mrs. Vickers, and who had stood by with a smirk when the decision was announced that Caro was to be banished from the family for all time. Georgiana was the one who had suggested Caro's name be struck from the family Bible. Thank God her mother had balked at taking things that far—it would have caused a horrific scandal—or Caro didn't know what would have become of her.

"Well, don't just stand there like a ninny," her mother

sighed. "Fetch your bonnet at once, child. We're expected at the Herrington's immediately."

For what felt like the dozent time in one conversation, Caro's heart dropped to her stomach and her stomach dropped to her knees. They didn't stay there, though. Both organs leapt with joy and hope, lodging firmly in her throat. It couldn't be. Rufus was the heir to an earldom and he was in search of a wife. Caro had never imagined Lord Barnabus Herrington, Rufus's father, would deem her capable of saving his family's fortune, but fate seemed to have stepped in. It seemed as though Caro was destined to repeat Jo's unaccountable luck and to have her wretched mother accidently engage her to precisely the right gentleman.

"I'll fetch it at once," she said, her voice hoarse as she turned and raced for the stairs. And if there were time, she would change her gown to something more fetching and pinch her cheeks until they glowed like roses. Although nothing could put a bloom on her face quite as determinedly as discovering true love was a mere carriage ride away.

CHAPTER 3

*L*ord Rufus Herrington felt like a caged bear as he stood behind the elegant sofa where his mother sat, reigning over a morning salon that felt more like a precursor to an execution than a polite social event.

"And do you suppose supplies of French lavender will be more readily accessible, now that the war has ended?" Lady Malvis Cunningham asked from her seat across the fashionable cluster of chairs and sofas from his mother. Her posture was rigid and her face was an expressionless mask of calm—far different from the vibrant cunning that lit Caro's eyes and with none of the splash of color that usually filled Caro's cheeks.

"One can only hope," Rufus's mother replied in a banal voice. "Just as one can only hope that certain elements of society will now return to their rightful places."

Rufus tried not to roll his eyes noticeably at his mother's comment. She had spent the last twenty years or more torn between her innate hatred of the French and her indignation that aristocracy of any sort could be treated as meanly as the Revolutionaries had treated French nobility. Now that the war was over, Napoleon was defeated, and Britain was seeking to restore France to its pre-Revolutionary status quo—something Rufus doubted would ever truly happen—the frogs, as his mother called them, could return to the continent and stop turning heads at London social events.

"At least we can be assured that French fashions will once again become dominant," Lady Andover, one of his mother's friends who had been invited to the unusual event said, then launched into a discourse about pelisses and sleeve styles.

Rufus would have pinched the bridge of his nose in frustration if he could have. There was a reason men and women did not generally take tea together of a morning. Ever since Lord and Lady Cunningham and Malvis had arrived, and shortly after the other guests—Lady Andover, and for some bizarre reason, Lord Hazelton—had joined Rufus and his parents in the large parlor, Rufus had wanted to crawl out of his skin and run. At least his father looked to be experiencing the same degree of torture. Although after the marriage his father was proposing for him, it served him right.

"One can only hope that the odious Mrs. Vickers will

stop publishing her scandalous stories now," his mother went on.

"Oh?" Lady Cunningham blinked rapidly, her cheeks going pink. "And why would she stop?"

"She is French, obviously," Rufus's mother said with a sniff. "Only a Frenchwoman would write such...." She sipped her tea rather than finishing her sentence.

"Yes, I suppose she is French," Lady Andover said. "Her stories do have a rather continental flare to them."

"Who is this Mrs. Vickers?" Rufus's father asked, interrupting his conversation with Lord Cunningham.

"An authoress," Rufus's mother said, then quickly added, "You would never have heard of her," with a wave of her hand.

"I've heard of her," Lord Cunningham said with a frown. "She writes salacious trash."

"And she makes a fortune at it," Lord Hazelton said. "Ruddy good stuff," he added with a look at Lady Cunningham that made her shudder in clear disgust.

"I find her work quite invigorating," Lady Andover said, fanning herself with one hand.

In fact, if Rufus had to wager, he'd bet that every woman in the room, including his mother, had read Mrs. Vickers's work. Every woman in London was talking about them. He'd indulged in a few of her books himself and found them quite inspiring. Of course, ever since Caro had nestled firmly in his heart, that inspiration had extended no further than his right hand, but he had every confidence that soon he would find a way to enact the things he'd read with the only woman he cared to imagine himself with for the rest of his life.

"When I am wed, I expect my husband to indulge my passion for French fashion," Lady Malvis said, changing the subject and sending a sharp, unsmiling, but blessedly brief glance in Rufus's direction and tumbling him out of his thoughts. "One's outward appearance is a reflection of one's inner standing, after all."

Rufus nodded, but only because he felt he was supposed to. Judging by Lady Malvis's outward appearance, she was as stodgy and grim on the inside as she was on the outside. She had the pale complexion of a young woman who deliberately avoided all sun and fresh air. Her gown was of fine material, but cut far too modestly for Rufus's taste. The neckline was indeed all the way at her neck. Not that it would do much good if it were lower. If Lady Malvis had breasts—and he was certain she must have had them in there somewhere, perhaps bound tightly to her narrow chest—they were hopelessly buried. The woman was all angles and thin lines. If he went through with his father's demands and married the woman, he had no idea how he would bed her. He couldn't help but imagine her breaking like a wishbone when he pried her legs apart.

"Do you not think so, Rufus?" his mother asked, jerking him out of his increasingly desperate thoughts.

"Yes, Mother," Rufus said with a nod, no idea what his mother was asking him.

She seemed satisfied and nodded. "As I said." She

turned back to Lady Malvis. "The Italian States are entirely unnecessary when visiting the continent."

Rufus clenched his jaw. In fact, he'd been to Florence once and enjoyed it thoroughly. He had a hankering to return to the Italian peninsula to explore more someday. Caro would certainly enjoy a holiday in the Mediterranean sun. He could imagine her decked out in Grecian costume, strolling about sunlit fields with one breast exposed. Or both. Or she could traipse through the meadows in the nude. He wouldn't mind. It was Italy after all.

"I bet I know what's put that spark in your cannon," Lord Hazelton said with a randy undertone, stepping up to Rufus's side.

Rufus dragged himself out of thoughts he would much rather have existed in, compared to the parlor where he actually stood, and stared hard at the older, ruddy-faced man. "I beg your pardon, my lord?"

"It's that tasty morsel of yours, isn't it?" Hazelton asked, wiggling his eyebrows. "That delicious Lady Charlotte or Catherine or some such?"

"I'm sure I have no idea what you are talking about," Rufus insisted even as his face grew hot. He glanced around the room to be certain no one was listening to Hazelton. Luckily for him, his mother and Lady Andover were still deep in whatever boring discussion they were having with Lady Malvis and her mother while Lord Cunningham and his father discussed business.

"Lady *Caroline*," Hazelton said in an entirely more

confident tone of voice. He made an appreciative sound that left Rufus wanting to throttle him. "She's a gem, that one, and I've known more than a few gems in my day." He laughed at his own joke.

Rufus's mother paused in the middle of her conversation to turn to Hazelton with an incredulous frown. Rufus clenched his jaw and drew Hazelton away from the circle of women and over to the side of the room.

"Lord Hazelton," he began in a tone that was admittedly too scolding for a young man to use with a more seasoned one. "I'm sure you are aware of the level of discretion involved in any activities engaged in at a revelry hosted by Mr. Khan."

"The tits on Lady Caroline, though," Hazelton said, grunting with lust and adjusting his breeches. "I meant what I said when I offered two guineas to have you tup her while she sucks my—" He had enough of a sliver of sense to glance back at the women instead of finishing his sentence.

"You never made such an offer, sir," Rufus told him, pretending he and Caro hadn't heard the disgusting man through the door while hiding. "I am offended that you would do so now."

"Come on, man," Hazelton said with a wry grin. "You and I both know which way the wind is blowing. And we know good and well what Khan's place is good for. I've found quite a few tasty morsels to add to my collection there. In fact, I think you'd be astounded to know about my latest acquisition which was discovered at Khan's house." He wiggled his eyebrows again.

Rufus's stomach turned, and he was on the verge of finding a way, any way, to put the man off, but a flash like lightning struck his mind. "Acquisitions?" he asked. "What do you mean by acquisitions? Are you a buyer of exotica?" And if he was, did he have something to do with the Chandramukhi Diamond?

"I have refined tastes," Hazelton said. "I collect whatever trinkets strike my fancy, the rarer the better."

Rufus's heart beat faster at the potential confession.

"I've had women of every shape, color, and description," he went on in an undertone, barely moving his lips as he spoke, as if trying to hide what he was saying from any prying ears. "That Indian princess Khan keeps in his house is an especially talented gem. I've had a whole crown full of them. But I am about to acquire the most precious gem of all, as I'm certain you'll agree."

Rufus's back prickled with revulsion and irritation. At the same time, he couldn't completely shake the thought that women were only one sort of gem Hazelton collected.

"Is this acquisition of yours—" he began, but was cut off as a flurry of activity marked yet another arrival to his parents' odd assembly.

"Ah, there's my crowning jewel now," Hazelton said, rubbing his hands together. "And I never would have thought to inquire after her if I hadn't seen how up for it she is, thanks to you."

Dread filled Rufus's stomach as he jerked toward the doorway to the parlor just as Caro stepped into the room.

CARO'S HEART WAS LIGHT AS A CLOUD AS SHE arrived at the Herrington's Mayfair house. She couldn't believe her luck, simply couldn't believe it. Her elation continued to lift her as the butler showed them into a parlor that was rather crowded with an odd assortment of men and women. Her mind skipped right over the unusual gathering as her eyes went straight to Rufus. She burst into a smile at the sight of him and was only slightly puzzled when the look Rufus sent her in return was one of horror.

"Ah, Lady Pepys," a middle-aged woman that Caro assumed was Lady Herrington greeted her mother as she stood. "How lovely of you to join us."

Intent on making a good impression, Caro turned to Lady Herrington, ready to curtsy with perfection and treat the woman with gratitude and affection. But the moment her gaze slipped past Lady Herrington to land on a sallow, sour-faced Lady Malvis, the butterflies that had been flitting happily in her stomach turned to stones that dropped into a pond of acid in her gut. Was she expected to somehow compete with Lady Malvis for Rufus's hand?

"Lady Herrington," her mother said, crossing to greet Lady Herrington in a faux embrace. "How good of you to host this auspicious gathering. As you know, my dear,

dear Georgiana is unwell at the moment and cannot abide visitors in our house."

Caro arched one eyebrow. That was the first she'd heard of her sister's health.

"I am only too glad to be of service," Lady Herrington said. "The occasion is perfect for Cupid's arrow to find its mark in more than one young person's heart." She glanced obviously between Lady Malvis and Rufus.

Caro's heart sunk along with her stomach. If her mother hadn't brought her to the Herrington's to announce her engagement to Rufus, then who—

"Lady Caroline, it is a pleasure indeed to see you looking so well."

A scream of protest threatened to rip from Caro's throat as none other than Lord Hazelton rushed forward to take her hand. She'd been so blinded by the gorgeous sight of Rufus that she hadn't noticed the aging lecher standing by Rufus's side. He grabbed her hand and raised it to his lips before she could shrink away from him, managing to make even that simple gesture feel as though he were thrusting a hand up her skirts.

"Lord Hazelton," she said, her voice coming out in a croak. She extracted her hand from his grip and turned to her mother. "What is the meaning of this?"

"Lord Hazelton has asked for your hand in marriage," her mother said, wearing a plastered-on smile that failed to reach her eyes. "Being heir to his father's earldom and an estate worth a king's ransom, of course your father and I could not refuse."

"Papa is ancient, the dear old man," Lord Hazelton said with laugh. "Refuses to give in, though. Still, I thought it wise to get a wife so that I can get an heir of my own before the yoke of responsibility falls on my shoulders. And seeing as I know we are of the same mind on so many things, the match will be perfection." He wiggled his eyebrows. It was an expression she'd seen him make far too many times at the East India Company's house. It put her off then and outright revolted her now.

"I'm certain we do not have much in common," she said in a low voice.

"Oh, but I know we do," he said in an equally low voice, as though they were alone instead of being watched by half a dozen people.

Unlike being observed in an intimate moment at one of Mr. Khan's parties—where a paradoxical understanding about observation, titillation, and discretion existed—Caro felt the scrutiny of Lady Herrington's guests as though they were High Court judges.

Caro cleared her throat, stepping closer to her mother and whispering, "I do not consent to this marriage."

Smile still firmly in place, her mother whispered back, "You will do as you're told."

Shaking with rage, Caro stepped back, clasping her hands tightly in front of her and sending Rufus a look as if to tell him she would find a way out of the mess. There was no point whatsoever in debating her mother in public. To do so would mean she ran the risk of being marched to the nearest chapel and wed to Lord Hazelton on the spot, never to return to the school—which she was coming to love—or her friends ever again.

"Tell us, Lord Hazelton," Lady Herrington said in a supremely diplomatic tone, gesturing for Caro's mother to sit on the closest sofa to her, "when do you plan to wed?"

"As soon as possible," Lord Hazelton answered. He attempted to sidle up to Caro's side, but Caro faked a coughing fit as an excuse to move to the edges of the room, closer to Rufus. That didn't dissuade Lord Hazelton from talking. "I have grand plans for my lovely bride. I intend to shower her with bridal gifts that will make a sultan jealous. Gems for my gem, after all. And then I plan to take her on a grand tour, not just of Europe, but of the world. We shall tour the far East and the West Indies. I will adorn her with exotic treasures on the island of Tahiti and in the courts of Imperial China."

Misery spread through Caro like a paralyzing illness. She would have loved to tour the world, but to do so as the prisoner of a man who she knew had diabolical sexual tastes would be torture. Perhaps literally. She would be separated from her friends, her publisher, from Rufus.

She snapped straight as the realization hit her. That was likely precisely why her mother had agreed to the horrid match.

Her irritation was so great that she almost didn't notice Rufus walking to the small table beside one of the sofas where tea was laid out. As the conversation turned to travel and a trip Lady Andover had taken to the island of Barbados, leaving Caro well on the outside of the group's focus, Rufus poured a cup of tea, then walked subtly to her side. She longed to speak to him, to share her fury at the way their parents were pushing their lives into disaster, but the rules of society dictated that she stop faking coughing fits and join the ladies in the inner circle.

She started to move when a deluge of warm liquid splashed over her arm and skirt.

"Oh dear, I am so terribly, terribly sorry, my lady," Rufus said as he righted the cup he'd just poured his tea out of. He rushed to place the cup on the tray containing the rest of the service, then dashed back to Caro's side. "Please forgive my clumsiness, though it is thoroughly unforgivable. Let me escort you downstairs so that our housekeeper, Mrs. Younge, can assist you in preventing any permanent stains to your gown."

Caro could have wept for joy and thrown her arms around Rufus's neck, but she knew there was a game to be played. "You, sir, are a vexing oaf," she said, even though it drew a shocked gasp from Lady Andover and a groan from her mother. "This must be remedied at once."

Rufus did a poor job of hiding the twitch at the corner of his mouth as he gestured for her to follow him out of the parlor. Caro went, listening for hints that the conversation had resumed without them and that they were quickly forgotten. Blessedly, that happened before they turned the corner and started down the hall.

Once they were alone, Rufus grabbed her hand and dashed down the hall, around the corner, down a servant's staircase, and into a room that appeared to be designated for polishing boots. He shut the door and turned the lock before rushing to take her into his arms. His lips slanted over hers in a kiss of pure desperation.

"This is a right mess," he said when he finished kissing her.

"I am so angry with my mother right now that I could scream," she said, still close to shaking with emotion.

"I know," Rufus said. "I braced myself for an explosion the moment Hazelton dared to take your hand."

"I will never marry him," she said, staring straight at him, determined to make certain he knew she was not the sort of milquetoast young lady who did whatever her parents said.

"If anyone can find a way out of a muddle like that, I'm sure you can," Rufus said, though truth be told, his confidence didn't reach his eyes.

Caro studied him. He didn't believe her. She could see it in him. He thought they were both doomed—him to marrying Lady Malvis and her to becoming Lady Hazelton. She had barely begun to fight, however.

"Are you engaged to Lady Malvis?" she asked, bracing herself for the worst answer.

"No," Rufus sighed. "There is no formal understanding in place, although there is an informal one."

"So you would not be subject to a lawsuit if you broke things off with her?"

"Not yet." He pulled her back into his arms, kissing her with a slow, burning passion. "You're the only woman for me, Caro. I've known it from the moment you ran headlong into me that night in Manchester Square."

In spite of her anger and anxiety, Caro's heart melted, she leaned into Rufus, splaying a hand across his chest to feel his pounding heart. "Do not give up hope yet, my love," she said. "Your beloved is far cleverer than most people know."

"And far naughtier," he added, closing a hand around her breast and teasing her nipple. "But I like a woman with a healthy appetite."

Caro laughed deep in her throat and lifted to her toes to kiss him. He accepted her with ardor, and within seconds, their kiss had turned into an intense mating of lips and tongues as their hands sought out each other's curves and hardness.

At least, until a loud knock sounded on the door.

"My lord," a deep, male voice said as Caro leapt away from Rufus. "Your father is deeply concerned about your and Lady Caroline's absence."

"Understood, Meyerson," Rufus said, then cleared his throat. He glanced regretfully at Caro. "We have to go back. It is already highly irregular to the point of comment for us to have scampered off like this."

"And I have so much more to tell you," Caro said, the haze of lust and disappointment lifting long enough for her to remember what had transpired that morning. "I may know where Miss Dobson has gone," she said. "In fact, I'm sure of it."

"And I have things to tell you about Lord Hazelton,"

Rufus said, the light of excitement returning to him as he unlocked the door and whisked her out into the servant's hall. "We have to speak, but how?"

Inspiration struck Caro, leaving a smile on her face. "Come to the school tonight. No one will question your presence, now that we have taken the school into our own hands."

"Surely someone will question it," Rufus said, one eyebrow arched doubtfully.

"Perhaps," Caro said, "but not enough to bar your entrance or to interrupt once we are alone."

Rufus grabbed her hand before they reached the stairs. "Are you saying you want to be alone with me, Lady Caroline?" he asked, fire in his eyes.

"Most definitely," Caro said in a deliberately sultry tone.

"Tonight it is then." Rufus glanced around to make certain they were unobserved, then whisked her into his arms for a thorough, yet all too short kiss. When he let her go he said, "Let me return to the parlor first. I'll act as though we rowed. Have Mrs. Younge escort you up in a few more minutes." He waved down the hall to a matronly woman, who nodded as if she were in on more than a few capers.

"Until tonight then," Caro said, kissing her fingers and placing them on his lips before he turned and dashed up the stairs.

CHAPTER 4

Somehow, Caro made it through the interminable morning's social call, but only by staying as far away from Lord Hazelton as she could manage in the cramped room. She insisted that her mother drive her immediately back to the school when the call was done or she would throw herself at Lord Hazelton the moment they stepped out onto the very public street.

"And I believe you know precisely how he would respond to such an action on my part," she whispered to her mother as they waited in the Herringtons' front hall for their carriage to drive around.

Her threat had teeth. The way her mother balked and went pale proved it.

"You will not disgrace me and our family name further by attempting to wheedle out of this match," her mother hissed in return. "I do not know how you have managed to have more of that filth published after the bribe—" She cleared her throat. "After your father had words with Mr. Prentice, but I am certain your husband will put an end to your outrageous activity the moment you are wed."

In fact, Caro had the oddest feeling that, if she were to go through with a marriage to Lord Hazelton, he would not only allow her to continue publishing, he would brag to all and sundry about her identity and claim he was the hero in all of her fiction. As delightful as it was to know her work had caused such a sensation, she was loath to let her true identity be known. At least, until the timing was advantageous.

By the time she returned to the school, a thousand minor matters required her immediate attention—not the least of which was changing her gown and handing the soiled one over to Flora to see if there was any hope of removing the tea stain. After that, she had to soothe Rev. Ellis's frazzled nerves in the wake of Felicity and Eliza filling his luncheon soup with tadpoles.

"It is the kind of prank I would expect from school-boys in short pants," Rev. Ellis complained in a huff, "not young ladies who should already be married and raising families of their own. I am not averse to instructing the pupils of this school," he went on before Caro could get a word in, "but I implore you to encourage your pupils to pursue that profession for which God intended them, that of wife and mother."

Caro thanked Rev. Ellis as graciously as she could

and insisted that suitable matches were the primary purpose of everything the school had to offer, but inwardly she seethed. Was that all women were to men? Vessels in which they could put their cocks, for propagation or for pleasure? Was a woman either a wife or a whore with nothing in between? She rejected the notion outright, but society, it seemed, was stacked against her.

Which was why, when Rufus arrived at the school as supper was adjourning, her spirits were not as excited as they could have been. Her mood dipped into even more dangerous territory when Rufus was forced to let himself in. When he stepped curiously into the doorway of the dining room without introduction and when the tables of chattering young ladies spotted him standing there—a handsome, young male of impeccable grooming, dressed in the latest fashion, with green eyes and fiery ginger hair —pandemonium erupted.

"Hello, sir."

The ladies closest to the doorway stood abruptly to greet him, peeling away from their tables and rushing to draw him deeper into the room. Most of the rest of the ladies stood and floated around him as Caro rolled her eyes and rose from her place at the head table. It was at these sorts of times that she missed Rebecca and Jo's friendships the most.

"Good evening, my lord."

"We are very pleased to see you."

"Isn't he handsome?"

"What delicious hair."

"And his arms are so strong."

Rufus glanced desperately at Caro across the sea of hungry young maidens who now handled his person. A glimmer of amusement filled his eyes at the attention he was getting, although it ended with an abrupt yelp. He jumped and twisted before asking, "Who just pinched my bum?"

A chorus of giggles and a second yelp from Rufus started a flurry of activity that would no doubt have ended in disaster if Caro hadn't reached the group, hooked her arm through Rufus's, and dragged him away from the ravening hoard and out into the hall.

"Go back to your supper," she called to the ladies over her shoulder. "And if you're so randy, seek out husbands." It wasn't precisely what Rev. Ellis had advised her to say or do, but it was close.

As Caro led Rufus down the hall, then up the stairs, thinking it wise to get him as far away from the rest of the ladies as possible, he let out a nervous laugh. "If you hadn't swept in, they would have had me for pudding," he said.

Judging by the fact that his jacket was unbuttoned, all but one of the buttons of his waistcoat were undone, and one side of the falls of his breeches hung open, he was probably right. His hair was disheveled and his cheeks bright pink to boot.

"I should hire them out to Mr. Khan," Caro laughed. "I can think of any number of men who would give their eye teeth to be savaged by a pack of ravenous schoolgirls."

Rufus's answering laughter was a mixture of amusement and dread. "They would go in expecting to play the master, but they would crawl out, naked, shaking, and dazed after being used within an inch of their lives."

Caro slapped a hand to her mouth as she led Rufus up to the second floor and on to her room. "They certainly would if Felicity and Eliza were in charge."

"Dare I ask who they are?"

Caro let Rufus into her room, followed him inside, then locked the door behind her. "It's best not to know," she laughed. "Besides, we have more interesting things to discuss."

Her heart flipped in her chest, and energy zipped through her as she met Rufus in the middle of the room, taking his hands.

"I believe I know where Miss Dobson is," she said.

"And I have strong reason to suspect that Hazelton's appearance in the room the night Felix and Josephine nearly caught the diamond thief was no accident," he replied squeezing her hand between them.

Caro's mouth dropped open. She hadn't expected her news to be trumped. "Why was he there?" she asked in a rush. "Is he culpable in the theft of the diamond?"

"I believe he is," Rufus said, triumph in his eyes. "Though I have no way to prove it as of yet."

A thousand additional questions popped into Caro's head. She searched back through all her memories of nights spent at the East India Company's house, reviewing what she thought she knew about Lord Hazelton. She'd written him off as nothing but a lecherous beast ready to do anything for pleasure, but had there been more to it? Had he attended Mr. Khan's parties for business purposes as well? He wouldn't have been the only one.

Instead of asking any of those questions, she shook her head and returned to what she needed to say before she forgot it entirely. "Miss Dobson is currently in residence at her father's country house."

It was Rufus's turn to look surprised, though his surprise switched quickly to thoughtfulness. "I suppose there is a degree of logic in that. The old duke always was fond of his by-blows. Heaven only knows he had enough of them. He's also been reported to be on his last legs."

"Do you think Miss Dobson is attempting to wheedle her way into his will?" Caro asked.

"Or to rob him blind when he's too ill to notice," Rufus said.

"How far from London is this house? We need to get to her before she slips out of our grasp once again."

"For what purpose?" Rufus said with a frown.

"To force her to implicate herself in the theft of the diamond, of course," Caro said, standing straighter in indignation.

A broad smile spread across Rufus's lips. "I love it when you're feisty," he said, slipping an arm around her waist and tugging her firmly against him. "You develop such a fetching blush."

"Are you certain now is the time to flirt?" she asked,

arching one brow, her will to resist him crumbling as fast as a sugar candy.

"Now is always the time to flirt," he said, his voice lowering to an amorous purr.

He slanted his mouth over hers, silencing any further protests she might have made. Within the blink of an eye, Caro forgot if she was planning to protest to begin with. His arms were warm and powerful around her. His heat infused her. His tongue teased hers, and he nibbled on her lower lip before drinking in another kiss that left her dizzy and throbbing. He closed a hand boldly around one of her breasts as well, kneading her through the muslin of her gown. Some women might have been alarmed at his greedy, roving hands and the speed with which they set to work, but she adored the way he fondled her and had from the start.

"We must seek out Miss Dobson and demand a confession," Caro sighed as Rufus relocated his kisses to her neck, then sucked on her earlobe.

"I will do anything you ask of me, my darling," he said, reaching behind her neck to tug at the ties of her gown. "As long as you do anything I ask of you."

A shudder of desire swept through her, pooling like flames in her sex. A man like Rufus could ask anything. She knew him well enough to know there was no limit to his imagination. Not only that, for the first time since they'd known each other, they were completely alone in a locked room with a bed, where Caro felt with absolute certainty they would not be disturbed. The chance she'd been waiting for since their first encounter in the dark street weeks ago was upon her.

"Ravish me, Rufus," she whispered, slipping her hands inside his jacket in an attempt to remove it from his shoulders.

Rufus sucked in a dazed breath and stood straight. "I beg your pardon?" he asked, blinking rapidly. His lips were swollen and his color high.

"We won't be disturbed," she said breathlessly, pushing his jacket off his shoulders. He shrugged it the rest of the way off and let it fall to the floor as she went on with, "I'm tired of waiting for you. I want to feel your skin against mine, your body encompassing me. I want to feel your stiff cock like a battering ram inside me."

He stared at her with incomprehension, barely breathing. She could see deep temptation in the depth of his gaze along with a good amount of confusion. "Do you," be began, swallowed, then stopped. His hands brushed her sides as though he were suddenly afraid to touch her. "Do you truly mean that?" Hope now danced along with the rest of the flames in his eyes.

"Do you doubt me?" she asked with a coquettish grin, lowering her eyes to watch as she plucked the last button free on his waistcoat.

"I know you have no objection to me playing with your baubles," he said, his smile returning as he raised his hands to mold her breasts into his palms. "And you did not object when I tickled your thighs and caressed your beautiful bottom at Khan's parties."

"Did you think it was all an act?" she asked, charmed by the sudden, new light that was being shed on his attentions and his character.

"I...." He blinked, reaching behind her to tug open the second set of ties holding her gown in place, then pulling her bodice down over her shoulders. Unfortunately for her, she was wearing sensible, concealing undergarments instead of the froth she wore at the East India Company's house. "I so hoped it was more than a game," he said in a low growl.

"I want you, Rufus," she repeated, wriggling out of her bodice as smoothly as she could and sliding her arms over his shoulders. Her fingers played through his hair. "I've wanted you in vivid, carnal ways right from the start. I want you to bend me and twist me and take me in every way you know how. And then I'll show you more ways to take me."

He let out a shuddering breath like a cry of mercy and brought his mouth crashing down over hers. This time, his ardor held an edge to it that made Caro's toes curl. He pulled frantically at her gown, urging it down over her hips and loosening her petticoats with it as he bruised her lips with his.

"Wait," he said a moment later, panting, taking a half step back. "Wait."

"Why?" Caro asked, tugging his shirt out of his breeches then slipping her hand below his waist to stroke his cock.

Rufus gasped and groaned and jerked his hips against

her. "If we continue like this, I won't be able to stop if you change your mind. I wish I could, but I'm not that strong and I need you too desperately."

"And where does the problem lie in that?" Caro asked reaching down to close her hands around his testicles.

He made another wild, pleasured sound before gasping out, "If you decide you want your virginity to remain intact—"

"It hasn't been intact for years."

He froze, his mouth dropping open. Caro swore she could feel his cock tighten in her hand at her confession.

"You're not—" he started to ask.

Caro shook her head and began to stroke him slowly. "Three years ago. In the country. At a house party. I was foolish and allowed myself to be compromised by a young buck on the prowl. He had no intention of marrying me. He already had his sights set on a widowed duchess and her fortune. But he was handsome, he was skilled, and I was eager and willing."

A jealous frown creased Rufus's brow, but he remained silent.

"I learned quickly how much I enjoy being bedded. And yes, I was flirting with unspeakable danger, but we were never caught and he did not get me with child. When the house party was over, we went our separate ways and haven't spoken since. And yes, I'll confess that I seriously considered taking another lover so that I could continue with an activity I enjoyed. But it wasn't possible. It was difficult enough to spend those weeks with him. A single, young woman has almost no time of her own, let alone time for assignations. Until now."

She increased the pressure of her hand stroking him and he reacted with an intake of breath and a shudder.

"So I run no risk of startling or offending you by hooking your ankles over my shoulders and fucking you hard and fast?" he asked, his eyes on fire as he met her gaze.

"Not a chance," Caro said, her heart speeding. "But do not be offended in return if I moan like a whore while you do it."

"My darling," he sighed, full of passion, and yanked her back into his arms.

His mouth ravaged hers, his tongue thrusting against hers to take what he wanted. But it was the work of his hands that left her breathless in no time. He tore at the laces of her stays as if impatient to have them gone. When they did finally drop to the floor as Caro shrugged out of them, he took hold of her thin, cotton chemise and tore it in two to expose her breasts. It was an unnecessary waste of a garment on the one hand, but the signal it sent was as essential as the blood pumping through her. He wanted her, and he would take her without holding back.

It was Caro's turn to whimper helplessly as he scooped her into his arms and lifted her, pressing her back into the wardrobe so that he could hold her at the right height to suckle her breasts. She rolled her head back against the wardrobe's hard surface, crying out softly as he stroked circles around one nipple, then sucked hard to bunch it into a sensitive pebble. She felt the pleasure of it all the way to her core. His breeches were loose enough that his enormous, hard cock stood straight up out of them, rubbing against her sex as he explored her breasts.

She reached up and gripped the top of the wardrobe while angling her hips deeper into his movements, then let out a long, pleasured sigh when the motion of his cock stroked her in just the right way. Combined with the way his tongue flickered over her nipple and his free hand squeezed her other breast, she was dangling on the precipice of orgasm in no time. He seemed to sense it as well and, with a surprise movement, he grabbed her thighs and shifted to slam deep into her.

Caro's eyes popped wide, and just as she'd promised, she moaned like a whore as his impossibly thick girth stroked deep within her. It was utter madness. She was naked and spread in the most ridiculous position, clinging to the wardrobe for dear life, and he was still dressed in his shirt, breeches, and boots as he fucked her. And there was nothing dainty or coy about his thrusts. He took her like a man who knew exactly what he wanted and had wanted it for a long time.

She shattered into orgasm, her body shuddering around him. He filled her so completely that there was hardly any room for her muscles to contract and milk him. The joy of it drove her senseless as pleasure throbbed through every inch of her body, leaving her panting and helpless. It was so good that even before the waves of pleasure slowed, she longed for it all to happen again.

It was only when Rufus pulled out of her and took a step back, lowering her to her shaky legs, that she realized he hadn't come yet. His jaw was clenched as if in complete focus and forced control, and his cock stood stiff and tall and now slick with her juices. Wordlessly, he stepped away from her, his breathing slow and deliberate, and peeled off his shirt. Caro had the vague sense that he'd come within a hair's breadth of spilling himself within her, but that he'd known when to stop and when to take a cooling step back so that he could keep going.

So that he could keep going. The idea reverberated through Caro's already sated body, igniting her all over again. She was awed by his control. She would have thrown herself on him, dropped to her knees and taken him deep into her mouth to finish him off, except that in doing so she felt she would cheat both of them out of what was a supreme effort on his part. So instead, she scrambled to her bed and threw back the covers before rolling onto her back and spreading her legs in a position of wanton submission.

"You're going to be the death of me," Rufus growled as he bent uncomfortably to pull off his boots.

"Over and over," Caro panted, resting one arm behind her head and playing with her breast with her free hand to tease him. "Now that I know what you're capable of, I'm never letting you go."

He discarded his boots and shoved his breeches down

over his hips, kicking them aside, and stood before her in all his aroused glory. "From your mouth to God's ears," he said in a rumbling voice. He stalked toward the bed with a look of such lust that Caro started shivering, then crawled on top of her, holding himself above her so that their flesh barely brushed. "Now that I know you're a thorough strumpet, I want you more powerfully than ever."

"Do you?" she asked, one saucy eyebrow arched.

"You have no idea," he said with a mix of need and seriousness. "I've had plenty of women, but I've never wanted one to swallow me whole as badly as I want you."

"That can be arranged," Caro said with a wicked grin.

She slithered down his body underneath him while he held himself on all fours until her mouth was at the level of his cock. With one hand cupped under his tightened balls, she drew his hard, hot staff to her mouth and closed her lips gently around the tip. He let out a half-hysterical groan as she teased his flared tip with her tongue, licking away the drop of moisture that had formed over its slit. Then, just to show him she could, she lifted her head and drew him in deep.

It was a shock to feel just how much bigger than her former lover he was. Drawing him all the way to the back of her throat wasn't easy. She had to let him go before she choked, but her point had been made. Rufus swore like a pirate as his entire groin tensed. He pulled his hips away from her, hinting that he was at the very edge of his remarkable control.

"Another day, perhaps?" she asked as she wriggled her way back to a more reasonable position under him.

He responded by rocking back and grabbing her knees only to lift them high and to the sides, laying her sex open fully for him. He wasn't sweet or gentle with her as he positioned himself perfectly to bring his mouth down between her legs. There was almost something vulgar in the way he raked his tongue across her weeping sex, as if her pussy were his to feast on. She gasped and gripped the mattress as he drove her hard and fast right back to the height of pleasure where he'd had her up against the wardrobe. It was as though he were demanding that she come again for him without shyness or giggles or any of the things that inexperienced lovers might play at while coaxing each other into orgasm. He wanted her at his mercy, and so she would be.

Her second orgasm tore through her like a wildfire, leaving her crying out with pleasure so intensely that not a soul in the house, or the entire square, could be in any doubt what was happening. Without him filling her, the throbbing was acute, leaving her sweating and gasping. And then he furthered his claim on her by thrusting deep inside of her before her shuddering climax was through.

It was raw, primal, and beautiful. He made desperate sounds of pleasure as he plundered her. She clasped her arms and legs around him, undulating with him and willing him to come as hard as she did. They were no longer a lord and a lady in proper British style, they were two virile creatures who had to mate with each other or die. She dug her nails into his back and buttocks, then burst into another wave of loud orgasm as he bit her shoulder. He finally came undone with a cry of triumph as her sex milked him. His body tensed and his thrusts grew pitched for a moment before slowing.

They collapsed, utterly spent, onto the damp and tangled sheets, barely able to catch their breath or extricate themselves from each other. Caro didn't ever want to unwrap her body from his. She would have been content to live in a constant state of semi-arousal, Rufus lodged within her, growing hard and soft in turn, over and over. All she wanted was to feel the heightened sense of pleasure and adoration that she felt in that moment. She loved him so dearly that it brought tears to her eyes, and she would fight for him until her last breath.

"We should—" she began to say through ragged breaths but was cut short, her blood suddenly running cold.

On the other side of the wall, slightly to the side of the wardrobe, came the sound of a male voice groaning in completion. Rufus tensed with a frown, but Caro knew in a heartbeat what had happened.

"Someone was watching us," she hissed. "From the secret passageway."

Rufus could only make an exhausted puzzled sound at first, but within a few seconds, the reality of the situation hit him and he snapped to full attention—or as much as was possible in a post-orgasmic haze.

"Secret passageway?" he managed to say as he wrenched himself to his knees above Caro. He scanned the room, growing ever more alert.

"You know about the secret passageway," she reminded him in a whisper, wriggling out from under him and standing. The warm stickiness that spilled down her thigh as she crossed to the wardrobe gave her a giddy thrill, but she was forced to push it aside as she reached for the wardrobe and tried to move it away from the wall.

Rufus was on his feet, moving the wardrobe for her, within seconds. "You didn't tell me there were peepholes into your room," he said.

"There aren't," she insisted. "Whoever that was must have just been listening."

The truth of the situation began to come into focus as the passion cleared from her brain. As soon as Rufus moved the wardrobe aside, she grabbed a candle from the bedside table and clicked the latch that opened the door to the passageway. Rufus took the candle from her and marched ahead. She had to grin over the fact that neither one of them seemed to be at all fussed by the fact that they were both naked and sweaty from making love. Time was of the essence, though.

A small, damp spot on the wall served as proof that whoever had been spying on them had climaxed, courtesy of Caro and Rufus's intimacy. What was less clear was which way he had gone. As usual, the secret passageway was dust free and tidy, so there were no foot-prints to indicate where the voyeur—if someone who only listened could be called that—had run to. Caro and Rufus moved along the passageway, searching for any hints as to their spy, all the same.

The closest they came to discovering who had over-heard them was a rumble of movement in one of the rooms on the same floor. Caro silently showed Rufus how the peepholes slid open and peeked into the room.

She nearly gasped aloud at the sight of Saif Khan fiddling with his breeches as though he was in the process of dressing or changing clothes. She jerked back from the peephole and beckoned Rufus to look as well. In the light of the candle, she saw him scowl, then lean away and shut the peephole. He then motioned for her to go back the way they'd come.

"It was Saif," he growled once they were back in Caro's room and the wardrobe had been moved to its proper place. "He must have been listening the whole time."

"We can't be certain of that," Caro said, though the knots in her stomach told her he had been. She chewed on her lip before glancing up to Rufus and asking, "Do you think he heard us talking about Miss Dobson and Lord Hazelton? And by the way, you still haven't explained your theory about Lord Hazelton to my satis-faction."

"I did other things to your satisfaction," he said with a rake's grin.

Caro felt herself begin to melt inside all over again. "If only there were time," she sighed.

Rufus seemed to grasp the seriousness. He rubbed a hand over his face and nodded. "We have to go to Kent to visit Miss Dobson at her father's estate," he said. "She's the lynchpin to all of this. Saif is involved as well. He might have just stumbled across information that will either help him abscond with the diamond or separate himself from the situation entirely."

"It could have been someone else listening in," Caro said because she felt she had to. "The East India Company house is crawling with male visitors in search of titillation these days."

"But do they know about the passageways?" Rufus asked.

Caro shook her head. "Most likely not. Rebecca, Jo, and I never encountered anyone else in all our explorations, most of which occurred before Saif Khan returned home."

"Then it had to be him," Rufus said, bending reluctantly to scoop up his clothing. When he straightened and donned his shirt he said, "I'll arrange transportation to Lord Somerset's estate as soon as possible. Will you be able to get away for an entire day?"

Caro grinned. "The school is more or less mine now. I can give myself a holiday if I choose."

"Good," Rufus said. "Then be ready, and soon."

CHAPTER 5

*I*t took a monumental amount of courage for Rufus to walk back into Caro's school two days after the evening of scandal he'd spent in her room. As it turned out, Saif Khan hadn't been the only one listening in on his amorous activities with Caro, as evidenced by the flurry of whispers that came from the hallway on the other side of the bedroom door just as the two of them had rolled back into bed instead of saying their goodbyes. Caro had donned her robe and stepped into the hall to have a word with her wayward pupils and friends, and when she returned, she'd advised Rufus to leave through the secret passageway instead of running the gauntlet of immoral heathens who had their ears pressed to the door and walls.

Two days was not enough to dampen the enthusiasm of the young ladies who were supposed to be reforming their characters instead of slipping further. The moment he stepped into the large dining room with its rows of tables, he was granted a standing ovation, led by Miss Felicity Murdoch and Lady Eliza Towers.

"Bravo," the two of them cried, encouraging the others to applaud as well.

Rufus had never felt the slightest bit of sheepishness over bedding a woman in his life, but as he glanced across the room to Caro, pleading with his eyes for her to hurry up so they could leave on their vital errand, his face glowed as red as his hair. He attempted to shush the cheering young ladies with a gesture, but they were determined to laud him to the high heavens.

"Are you a zookeeper, madam?" he asked Caro once they were safely in the carriage he'd commandeered from his father's fleet for their errand. "Those ladies—if they can be called that—are a pack of wildcats."

"They are," Caro said with a proud smile.

Rufus loved her and was baffled by her in equal measure. "You know that none of them will be given even a scrap at the table of polite society if so much as a hint of their behavior is made public, don't you?"

Caro grew more serious. "None of them stood a chance of being accepted by the *ton* to begin with. And I fear that most of them will meet a scandalous end, one way or another."

"Then why let them carry on so?"

She turned to him with an incredulous look. "Because there are more ways to live than those approved of by the *ton*. There are more futures to be had than those as wife to a respectable, stodgy man and mother of his children. The sun rises and sets each day for the unconventional as well as for those who follow the rules."

"But any path other than the expected is a hard one to walk," he said.

"Which is precisely why I work so hard to give my friends the skills they will need to fight as they travel that path. We do not all wish to be proper showpieces in careful, controlled studies of the perfect English family, you know." She tilted her chin up in challenge.

A smile spread across Rufus's face that seeped all the way into his soul. He brushed his fingertips across the softness of her cheek. "That is why I love you, you know." Her blush deepened and her eyes glittered with surprise and affection. "With you, I can be as mad and bad as I want to be and you won't deride me for it."

"You wish to be mad and bad, then?" she asked, arching one brow.

"So very much," he said in a low growl, leaning into her and slanting his mouth over hers.

The drive to Kent was sufficiently long enough for him to prove just how mad and bad he could be. It was long enough for Caro to prove how nubile she was as well. The jostling of the carriage as it traveled roads of questionable condition was enough for the two of them to expend surprisingly little energy as she straddled him, his cock buried deep in her slippery sheath.

By the time they reached the modest grounds of Somerset's country house—not to be confused with his vast landholdings in the county of Somerset from whence his title was derived—both Rufus and Caro were disheveled, sweaty, and thoroughly spent. Somehow, they managed to pull themselves together enough to stumble out of the carriage and approach the front door.

A butler who appeared to be as old as the duke himself answered the door. Rufus drew himself to his full height—in spite of the fact that his hair was a mess and his lips were a tinge too red and swollen for innocence—and asked, "Is Miss Dobson at home?" as though they were on a banal social call instead of a dire investigation.

"Who shall I say is calling?" the butler said in a voice like ancient, crumpled paper.

"Lord Herrington and friend," Rufus told him. There was an outside chance Miss Dobson wouldn't quite know who that was and would be curious enough to allow them in.

"One moment, my lord," the butler said with a deep bow. He showed Rufus and Caro into a waiting area just inside the front hall, then disappeared into a side room.

"This is encouraging," Caro whispered, standing close enough to Rufus to reach for his hand and squeeze it.

"Agreed," he whispered back. "We can only hope the rest of the meeting is as auspicious."

A moment later, Miss Dobson stepped out of the room the butler had ventured into. Caro's jaw nearly dropped. The woman had undergone a complete trans-formation. Instead of the haughty schoolmistress in serviceable muslin, wearing a cap, Miss Dobson appeared to be a grand lady, completely at home in a wealthy household. She wore a gown of deep blue brocade In a style that might have been fashionable when she was a younger woman and her hair was topped with a stylish turban. She carried herself with a serene grace and her expression was one of smooth boredom.

At least until she spotted Rufus and Caro.

All at once, everything noble about her dropped into open-mouth shock. Her eyes grew wide with panic. "No," she said, taking a few steps back. "I am not at home to these people. Evans, get rid of them."

Rufus wasn't about to let a butler as old as Methuselah put him off. He marched after Miss Dobson when she retreated into the parlor just off the hall, Caro right behind him.

"We are not here to take up your time," he said without addressing Miss Dobson, either as a friend or a superior. She was neither as far as he was concerned. "We merely have questions."

"I don't know anything," Miss Dobson insisted, retreating to the far end of the room and slipping behind a large chair, as though it could defend her.

"Lies will merely prolong this process," Caro said, coming to stand boldly by Rufus's side. "Where is the Chandramukhi Diamond?"

Rufus had to admire her courage and directness. He would show her just how much once they returned to London.

"I know nothing," Miss Dobson repeated. "Leave me alone."

"You were present in the same room with the thief on the night Lord Lichfield nearly unraveled the theft," Rufus said. "You cannot pretend innocence now."

"It was a coincidence," Miss Dobson insisted, everything from her expression to her posture proving her words to be a lie. "A mere coincidence."

"Evidence of your guilt was found at the school after your departure," Caro said, taking a threatening step forward.

Rufus did his best to hide his surprise. He couldn't tell if Caro was bluffing or if there was something she hadn't told him. Of course, he lived in a constant state of feeling there were things she hadn't told him.

Whatever her intentions, they worked. Miss Dobson's lips quivered, and she sagged against the chair. "All right," she said in a mournful voice. "I'll tell you what I know, but it isn't much."

She glanced to Caro, then Rufus, as though waiting for them to make some further comment. They both remained silent, staring intently at her and waiting.

Miss Dobson's shoulders sank and she let out a dramatic sigh. "I am not the thief," she said. "Wallace Newman is."

A surge of victory shot through Rufus's gut. He'd known it. He'd known it all along.

Miss Dobson went on. "He was there that evening to sell the diamond to Lord Hazelton."

Caro sucked in a breath, snapping straighter and twisting to meet Rufus's eyes. Prickles of surprise shot down Rufus's back, numbing his hands with shock. He shouldn't have been surprised that Hazelton was involved, not after the things he'd said the other day, but somehow, he was. It all fit into place, though.

"He wasn't there to pursue Jo and Felix," Caro whispered, pressing a hand to her stomach.

Rufus nodded, understanding fully what she'd meant. The man was a libertine and a blackguard. Unfortunately, as the sale hadn't taken place, he wasn't a criminal. Not yet.

"That is all I know, I swear," Miss Dobson wailed, dabbing at her eyes with a handkerchief she pulled from one of her sleeves. "Now leave me alone."

"Not yet," Caro said, turning her scrutiny back on the woman. "What about Saif Khan? How is he involved?"

"Saif Khan?" Miss Dobson's face flushed a deep shade of red and she seemed to shrink in on herself. "I don't know. I don't know anything about him."

"Be careful of lying, madam," Rufus said. "Lies never help the liar in the end."

"I am not lying," she insisted unconvincingly. "I know nothing about the man."

"He was in the room during the evening in question," Rufus reminded her.

"I swear, I do not know why," Miss Dobson blurted, annoyingly genuine. "Perhaps he was Wallace's accomplice. Perhaps he was connected to Lord Hazelton in some way. He is the son of the man who hosts the parties, is he not? Perhaps he was attempting to cheat his father in some way. Fathers and sons despise each other. Or perhaps he merely wanted to bribe the partygoers. You know that savage Indians cannot be trusted."

Rufus clenched his teeth, his nerves bristling. He didn't trust Saif as far as he could throw him, but the man was far from savage. Every one of the gentlemen from the subcontinent that he'd met were as civilized and educated as any other man.

"Your prejudices will do you no good, madam," he told Miss Dobson, "and your lies will not save you in the end."

"I am not a liar," Miss Dobson insisted, raising her voice. She glanced to Caro. "If you want to know a liar, there she is." She flung an arm toward Caro, one bony finger pointed.

"I beg your pardon?" Caro yelped.

"She's the liar," Miss Dobson insisted, narrowing her eyes and glancing back to Rufus. "I can tell you are enamored of her, but she is full of lies and deceptions. She stinks of them. Just ask her. Ask her about her wickedness and about her lies, the little strumpet."

Rufus grinned as though he didn't care one wit about the accusations. "Caro and I have no lies between us," he insisted.

"No?" Miss Dobson stood straighter. "No doubt she's played the blushing virgin with you. She is no such thing.

You would be a fool if you cast your lot with her. Her secrets are numerous and wicked."

"You do not know half of my secrets," Caro told the woman, shoulders squared, head held high. "Come along, Rufus. I think we've learned all we need to know here."

Caro turned to go. Rufus followed. Caro was right, they knew all that Miss Dobson had to tell them now. Everything else was unimportant.

"She's a whore," Miss Dobson called after them. "Just ask her. Ask Mr. Prentice."

Rufus couldn't stop his brow from jerking up, but he refused to pause or turn around and ask Miss Dobson what she meant. The woman was bitter and would say anything.

All the same, once they were back in the carriage and rolling along the road back to London, he turned to Caro and asked, "Mr. Prentice?"

Caro merely laughed and shook her head.

A twist of surprising jealousy gripped Rufus's gut. "Is he your former lover?" The image of Caro naked and splayed while another man pleasured her into the sounds he'd provoked her to make two nights ago burned in his mind.

"You truly have no reason to be alarmed by a weak accusation such as Miss Dobson's," she said, cradling the side of his face with one gloved hand.

"But is he?" Rufus repeated, one brow arched.

Caro grinned mysteriously at him, but said, "No. No he is not." She shuddered, then added, "Never."

"Then who is the man?" Rufus's mind began to turn with all the ways he could pry the truth out of her.

"He is unimportant," she said with a saucy roll of her shoulders and the light of mischief in her eyes. "All that is important now is contacting Nigel Kent and the rest of the Bow Street Runners to tell them Miss Dobson has given us the name of the diamond thief. Frankly, I knew it was Mr. Newman all along."

She was barely able to finish her sentence before Rufus pulled her across his lap and planted a searing kiss on her open mouth. As he did, he unbuttoned her pelisse and pushed it off her shoulders so that he could fumble for the ties holding her gown together in back. She sighed into their kiss, doing nothing at all to impede his mischief, even though she must have known his intent. He was able to loosen her bodice and the top of her stays enough to scoop her breasts out into the open.

"Are you a whore?" he asked mischievously as he rubbed his palms against her nipples to harden them.

"I think you know the answer to that," she said breathlessly, undulating against him in a way that encouraged him to manhandle her.

His pulse raced and his cock hardened. The carriage was cramped and their position painfully awkward, but he couldn't bring himself to care at all. He kissed her again, punishingly, thrusting his tongue against hers as a way to show her that she was his and his alone. He reached for the hem of her skirt, clumsily bunching it around her waist so that he could slip his hand along her leg. He hooked a hand under her knee, lifting it in a way that opened her hips.

"Only an irredeemable strumpet would let a man do these things to her in a speeding carriage," he panted, teasing his fingers along the hot flesh of her thigh.

"As you say," she said with a devilish grin.

Her bottom nestled temptingly against his groin while the rest of her was splayed wantonly across him and the seat. Her pelisse slipped to the floor and her firm, glorious breasts spilled over the top of her sagging bodice, on full display for him. Her skirts were gathered above her waist and one leg was fully exposed while the other was mostly exposed. All he had to do was bunch the fabric a little more and her sex would see the light of day. He was utterly certain it would be glistening with her wetness and pink with anticipation. And to top it all, she wore a supremely wicked grin, as though daring him to pleasure her until she came for him.

She was astoundingly wanton, shockingly immoral. She would be shunned by anyone who considered themselves good or upright. They would call her far worse than a whore, cut her at every opportunity, and cast her off as a condemned soul. If they could see her. If they found out. Rufus burned for her. No woman had ever excited him so much, had ever made him feel as though he wanted to live in a constant state of arousal, fucking, coming, and recovering as fast as possible so that he could do it again. Her very wickedness was what drew him to her, particularly the way she hid it so well when she was in polite society.

He brushed his hand up her thigh, burying his two middle fingers deep in her dripping pussy and clasping the rest of his hand around her sex as she gasped and squeezed him.

"This is mine," he said, not caring how rough or possessive he sounded.

"Did they not teach you anatomy at university," she sighed, flexing and grinding against him to pleasure herself. "I believe the part you have laid claim to belongs to me." She met his eyes with a look of ferocity.

She was going to be the death of him. His cock ached so much that he fumbled to unfasten the falls of his breeches to free himself with one hand while the other stayed lodged firmly where it was. The open air was little relief, though. Nothing but sheathing himself within her would satisfy him, but he wasn't ready yet.

He ground the bottom of his hand against her clitoris while his fingers stayed lodged inside her. "Do you think of him when you come?" he asked, letting himself be jealous to increase the intensity of emotion pounding through him.

"What do you think?" she asked, panting and gasping as she moved into his touch.

Their position was strange enough that he was able to bend forward and nip one of her nipples with his teeth. She let out a cry and tilted her head back, jerking harder against his hand.

"I think you want it," he growled, stroking his fingers against her inner walls. "I think you're wild for it."

"I am," she confessed in a hungry voice.

His groin tightened, and he had to fight not to come at the sight of her twitching and writhing as she came close to climax.

"I think you would do any number of dirty things for me, and you would like them," he went on.

"I would," she gasped, her breath coming in such short gasps and groans that he expected to feel her throbbing at any moment.

"I think you long to be a wicked, wicked whore, but only for me."

She responded by bursting into orgasm. She cried out sensually as her inner muscles throbbed and contracted around his hand. Her face contorted with pleasure—pleasure he had given her—and she flushed a deep shade of scarlet. Her orgasm went on and on, and he stroked and rubbed her to keep it going as long as possible.

When it was finally done, her body went soft and fluid, but he was as hard as a pillar. His groin ached so desperately that a gentle breeze could have made him come. But he was hardly going to spend for a breeze.

He nudged her off his lap and pushed his breeches over his hips, lifting his shirt out of the way so that his cock jerked truly free and his balls tightened in the cool air. But he didn't stop there. He grabbed Caro around the waist, bringing her back to him, though she faced the front of the jostling carriage. He would have taken her in the ass if he'd had something slick on hand, but her glorious quim was slick enough.

He brought her down hard on his cock, jerking his hips to sheath himself in her to the hilt. She let out the most sinfully delicious cry as he impaled her and tilted her hips to take him in more fully. It was wild, untamed, but amazing. She arched her body, moving with him as he pounded into her as though she were a cannon and he was a ramrod. His only regret was that he couldn't see her tits joggling as he fucked her. He settled for reaching for them and closing his hands around them as they moved.

He wanted it to go on forever. Every inch of him felt alive. His heart was full nearly to bursting at her willingness, her adventurousness, at the way she made him feel like he was the most desirable thing in the world. So desirable that she was willing to ruin herself just to have him blow his seed inside her. She wanted him that much. She was the only person in his life who had ever wanted him so desperately as to be reckless. She would love him forever just as he was.

That thought started the chain reaction that contracted his groin and sent liquid heat searing through him. He came hard, crying out her name as he did. The pleasure of it was beyond compare, and even after his essence had left him and the will to move began to ebb, joy continued to tingle through him.

They stayed in their awkward position, his softening cock still inside of her, for what should have been an embarrassingly long time. It felt so good just to be joined with her. Even when she finally righted herself, primly straightened her skirts and collapsed onto the seat beside him, snuggling against his side and tucking his cock back into his breeches, the joy lingered.

"Let's run away together," he said softly once he'd caught his breath. "Forget Lady Malvis and Lord Hazelton, diamonds and thieves. Forget everything. Let's make a new life together in...in Australia."

"Let's make a life together here," she countered with a happy sigh, resting her head against his shoulder.

"We can't," he said, his stomach pinching at the thought.

"Can't we?"

Her clever answers would drive him mad, but at least he would be happy in his madness.

He fell asleep, his head lolling against the back of the seat, not long after that. In the back of his mind, he wasn't certain if he'd fastened his breeches properly, and he knew his shirt hung loose. It didn't seem to matter one bit, though.

At least, not until a loud knock on the carriage door roused him—and Caro, who had also fallen asleep—from slumber. Rufus snapped his eyes open and jerked his head up. When had the carriage stopped?

"Rufus." His father's sharp voice sounded through the door a moment before the door in question was thrown open.

Light spilled into the dim carriage interior. In an instant, Rufus noted that, in fact, he hadn't properly fastened his breeches. He hadn't fastened them at all. Worse, his penis poked from the side of the hastily-arranged fabric. He wasn't the only one in disarray. Caro's breasts were still on full display. His father stared furiously at the two of them. There could be no doubt at all in the man's eyes about what had happened.

"Pull yourself together and exit that carriage immediately," the old man growled in dangerous tones.

Rufus sent a wary look to Caro, who was suddenly fully awake. He did his best to make himself partially presentable as she did the same. He then gestured for her to stay where she was as he exited the carriage.

"Father, I can expl—"

"Who you keep as your mistress is none of my business," his father cut him off.

Rufus's brow shot up at the surprisingly magnanimous comment, but his father wasn't done.

"Discretion," he hissed. "The carriage has been sitting here in the mews for the past twenty minutes. It sat in front of the house for ten before Bullard had the intelligence to drive out of public view."

"I'm sorry," Rufus said, merely because he could think of nothing else to say.

His father's scowl deepened. "I cannot stop you from taking whoever you want to bed," he said, "but you will do your duty to your family all the same. Lady Malvis is anxious for a proposal, and you will give it."

Rufus's frustration and disappointment must have

showed on his face. His father's expression softened to a sigh of regret.

"I'm sorry for all this, son," he said, shaking his head. He glanced back to the carriage, where Caro was watching through the open door. "Under other circumstances, Lady Caroline would be a reasonably suitable match and I would give my blessing wholeheartedly, especially considering the insult to her honor that you have perpetrated." He leaned closer. "But her family has no money. Her dowry is minimal. We must make these sorts of decisions with our heads not our—" He pressed his mouth shut and let out a breath, leaving Rufus wondering if he would have finished with "cocks" or "hearts".

"I understand, Father," Rufus said. "As long as you understand that Caro will forever be a part of my life."

His father looked even sadder. "You'll have a hard time of that once Hazelton gets his claws in her. Joseph Pepys is a villain for handing his daughter over to a satyr like that."

It surprised Rufus more than he could say that his father agreed with him. Maybe the old man wasn't so bad after all. But if he wasn't, the situation they both found themselves in was.

"Tomorrow," his father said. "I've arranged for you to walk out with Lady Malvis in Hyde Park. You will propose to her then and make this match official."

"But, Father—"

"I'm sorry, son, but this is the way it has to be," his

father cut off his protest. "Now, see to your lover. Get her home before either of you are noticed. And if you wish to keep any sort of connection to her, move heaven and earth to ensure that you are not seen together until both of your positions are secure."

CHAPTER 6

*R*ufus expected to lay awake all night, trying to find a way out of proposing to Lady Malvis in the morning. That or racking his brain for ways that he and Caro could expose Wallace Newman as the diamond thief and bring him and Lord Hazelton to justice. But after returning Caro to her school, enduring a painfully long supper with his family, and dragging himself up to his room after midnight, the moment his spent body hit his bed, he fell asleep. It shouldn't have come as a surprise, considering how "active" he and Caro had been during their carriage rides.

His dreams were filled with astoundingly carnal images of Caro riding him like a thoroughbred, and he awoke with a smile and a cockstand. But that happy state of being faded fast when reality swooped down on him.

"You are expected at Cunningham House at precisely ten this morning," his father reminded him at

81

the breakfast table without looking up from his ham and eggs. "Dress appropriately for this weather and make your suit clear and concise."

"Yes, Father," Rufus grumbled. He'd helped himself to a large breakfast, but the food seemed to turn to ash in his mouth after a few bites. He pushed his plate back and stood, marching out of the room without another word for his parents or his brother. If he was doomed to engage himself to a woman he could never love and to throw over the one woman whom he ached to spend the rest of his days with, he might as well get it over with as soon as possible.

The one light of consolation in the whole mess was that he had just enough time to send Nigel Kent a missive detailing his and Caro's interview with Miss Dobson the day before. There was no telling if Kent would believe him, though. As far as he knew, Kent still saw him and Felix Lichfield as the prime suspects in the theft. Attempting to help the investigation couldn't hurt, though.

By the time he rolled to a stop in front of Cunningham House and dragged himself up to the front door to inquire after Lady Malvis, he was restless and irritable and considering throwing himself in the Thames to avoid what he knew he had to do.

"You're late," Lady Malvis snapped after introductions and pleasantries directed to her mother, once the two of them were strolling along Brook Street toward Hyde Park, arm in unfortunate arm.

"I don't believe I am," Rufus said with a frown.

"You arrived at three past ten," Lady Malvis informed him.

Rufus clenched his jaw. "I would hardly call that late."

"I would." The two words were as sharp as a switch to the knuckles delivered by a particularly vicious governess. But Lady Malvis wasn't done. "When we are wed, I will expect perfect punctuality in all things."

Rufus remained silent and sullen. He supposed Malvis would set a strict schedule for the marriage bed as well. He would be required to come after ten strokes precisely, not nine, not eleven. And if he failed to impregnate her immediately, he would be forced to stand in the corner reciting scripture until he mended his ways.

"You are too quiet," Lady Malvis scolded him when they crossed into the park and began to stroll along one of the many paths toward the Serpentine. "A gentleman should be practiced in the art of polite conversation."

He would have sighed in exasperation if he didn't think that would have drawn more censure from his bride-to-be. She was probably fishing for him to propose immediately. Well, at least he had some control over that. He would make her wait as long as possible.

"The weather has been fine for so late in the season," he said, a stubborn set to his shoulders.

"It has," Lady Malvis said with an irritated pinch to her lips. "With Christmas in a matter of weeks, one wonders if it will feel as festive as it should."

He darted a sidelong look at her. Was that another prompt to get it over with?

Before he could decide on an answer, a rolling peel of feminine laughter snagged his attention. He glanced ahead to the banks of the Serpentine only to see a large cluster of young ladies bundled in winter coats and bonnets. They were the pupils from Caro's school. Most of them were seated on benches, a few in the cold grass, with books that were apparently fascinating. Interspersed among them were a few ladies standing before easels with small canvases fixed to them. And prominent in their midst was Caro herself, dressed in a cheery coat of berry red, a bonnet decorated with Christmas greenery atop her blonde hair. His heart leapt to his throat, then dropped to his feet, in an instant.

"What a curious and inappropriate activity for young ladies on a morning such as this," Lady Malvis sniffed.

"I find it a fine and healthy activity for excitable young minds, such as the pupils of Miss Dobson's school have," Rufus said, his voice slightly raised in irritation.

His irritation was nothing to the peevishness with which Lady Malvis turned to him. "Miss Dobson's School?" She huffed as though inmates from the Tower had been let loose on the lawn.

It was at that moment that Caro stepped back from examining the painting one of her friends was working on and glanced at Rufus. Their eyes met so fast that there wasn't a single doubt in Rufus's mind that she'd been aware of him from the moment he stepped into the park.

Even with the distance between them, he could see the mischief in her eyes and the sly grin that tugged at the corners of her mouth—a mouth that tasted of life and adventure and had molded to his as if they were meant to be one.

"I think it is a supremely admirable thing for young ladies to be educated," he told Lady Malvis, more confrontation in his voice than he should have had.

As expected, Lady Malvis scoffed. "Educating women is as useful as throwing pearls before swine."

Rufus frowned at her wholly unoriginal metaphor and the motivation behind it.

"Besides," Lady Malvis went on, narrowing her eyes at the young ladies. "Everyone knows that Miss Dobson's is no mere school." The derision with which she spoke left no doubt in Rufus's mind that Lady Malvis was a snob and a prude. But he was truly enraged when she went on with, "A list of students from that wretched institution has circulated among influential members of the *ton*, and it has been agreed that they will not be known under any circumstances. Neither will anyone who breaks the vow of exclusion be known."

"What do you mean?" Rufus growled.

"I mean that if you—that is to say, if anyone who wishes to have a place in polite society so much as acknowledges any of those young ladies, they will be cast out thoroughly."

In spite of the shocking meanness of Lady Malvis's words, hope soared in Rufus's chest. Could it be that all he had to do was bid Caro and her friends good day and the Gorgon would throw him over as unworthy? He was desperate to give it a try.

But before he could steer Lady Malvis onto a path that would intersect with Caro and her lot, disaster struck. Or as close to disaster as Rufus felt it was possible to get. He wasn't the only one interested in striking up a conversation with Caro. Oh, no. Before he could so much as blink, none other than Lord Hazelton came strolling up the path and up to Caro's side.

The rage that flared through Rufus was so hot that he stopped in his tracks and narrowed his eyes at the old lecher. His reaction did not go unnoticed, of course.

"Whatever is the matter?" Lady Malvis hissed impatiently. She followed the line of his gaze and huffed. "Why should you care if a gentleman of such ill-repute as Lord Hazelton passes the time of day with that lot?"

Rufus didn't answer. He couldn't have if he'd wanted to. Lord Hazelton had just leaned into Caro to whisper something in her ear.

EVERYTHING WAS GOING PRECISELY TO PLAN AS FAR as Caro was concerned. The young ladies were more than happy to have their lessons in the fresh air of Hyde Park, in spite of the nip in the air. Rufus and Lady Malvis had arrived precisely when she expected them to, based on what she'd overheard Lord Herrington tell Rufus the day before. And Felicity and Eliza were ready and waiting with their plot to distract Lady Malvis so that she could prevent Rufus from proposing as his father wanted him to. She would have preferred to wait and reveal her grand plan to save the Herrington fortune in a more dramatic style, but she was willing to settle for a lower level of drama, now that Rufus's back was against the wall. She had a copy of her latest book in hand and a letter from her publisher detailing her most recent royalties ready to show as proof that she would bring far more wealth into a marriage than Rufus or his father could imagine.

The plan would have worked like clockwork if Lord Hazelton hadn't shown up.

"My dear Lady Caroline, you are looking lovely today," he said as he veered off the path and marched boldly up to her.

Every nerve in Caro's body tensed, but not for the reasons many would have assumed.

"Lord Hazelton," she said with a plastered-on smile, stepping away from Ophelia as she worked on her painting to greet him. "How...interesting to see you today." She couldn't bring herself to lie, not even for the sake of politeness, to tell him it was pleasant to see him.

"The surprise and delight are all mine," Lord Hazelton said, sliding far too close to her. "If I had known you would be here this morning, I would have brought you a little treat to nibble on." He swiveled his hips in a way that made it all too clear what his meaning was.

"Little?" Caro asked, one eyebrow raised.

Lord Hazelton's face went red. "Well, not so very little," he said clumsily. "Tasty all the same and quite to your liking, I'm sure."

Caro clenched her jaw, not out of disgust—though she felt plenty of that—but because she had to force herself not to spew out a string of withering put-downs. Lord Hazelton was there, right in front of her. The man who had attempted to buy the Chandramukhi Diamond, according to Miss Dobson, may have walked right into her web. If she could finagle a confession out of him....

"What does bring you to Hyde Park this morning, my lord?" she asked, taking a risk and looping her arm through his to walk him away from her girls.

She sent a glance to Felicity and Eliza as they sat poring over her latest book. The two women nodded and leaned toward each other to whisper plans.

"I'm here to meet friends," Lord Hazelton said, then rushed on with, "But I am so much happier to have met you, my darling, my love, my future wife. I have not yet set a date with your father, but I was thinking—"

"Lord Hazelton," Caro cut him off. She darted a glance farther down the path to where Rufus and Lady Malvis stood, apparently bickering now. Rufus glanced in her direction. "You do realize that my opinion in the matter has not been sought."

Lord Hazelton shrugged. "It has never been truly necessary to secure a woman's opinion in matters of marriage. You all want the same thing." He executed one of his ridiculous eyebrow wiggles.

"And what, pray tell, is that, my lord?" she asked in a flat voice.

"A husband," he said as though it were the most obvious thing in the world. "Children. Scads of them. And wealth too, if you can get it. I can give you all those things and more."

"More?" Caro asked, her voice even flatter.

Lord Hazelton chuckled lasciviously and leaned closer to her—so close that it elicited a shocked gasp from a pair of middle-aged women passing them on the path. "I can give it to you the way you like it—hard and dirty. I won't even protest if you want it from half a dozen other men as well. In fact, I'd pay good money to watch you used by five men at once. It can be done, you know, one the standard way, one up the ass—"

"Lord Hazelton, stop at once," Caro shouted, far too loudly and vehemently for Hyde Park. He had genuinely enraged her, though. To the point where she shook from head to toe. Just because she enjoyed sex with one man—one dear, beloved, particular man—didn't mean she was a slut without limits. That he would assume she was based on observing her at play with Rufus was unforgivable. "You go too far," she hissed, lowering her voice once more.

Rufus had witnessed the entire exchange, though. It was as plain as day that he could read her expression and knew Lord Hazelton had overstepped his bounds. His face was as dark as a thundercloud, and in spite of the fact that Lady Malvis had a hold of his sleeve and appeared to be chastising him for one thing or another, his gaze was locked on Caro. Or rather, on Lord Hazelton. Within moments, he'd broken away from Lady Malvis and was storming toward them.

For good or bad, that appeared to be Felicity and Eliza's cue for whatever mischief they were plotting. As Lady Malvis let out a yelp and swayed forward, as if she would chase after Rufus and drag him back to her side, they zipped along the path to intercept her.

"Lady Malvis Cunningham, is that truly you?" Eliza began their ruse.

That was as much of the show as Caro was able to watch. Rufus was closing in on her and Lord Hazelton, but Lord Hazelton hadn't noticed yet.

"Come now, my dear," he said, attempting to brush Caro's arm in what he must have foolishly thought was a soothing manner. "I am a man of the world. I know that not all women are blushing violets. Why do you suppose I asked for your hand in particular? At last, I have found a woman whose tastes match my own. I will deny you nothing as my wife, not even behind closed doors. I will shower you with jewels. I have my eye on a particularly fine wedding present for you. I would—"

He stopped, not because Caro cut him off or because Rufus intervened. Rufus was still a few yards off. No, Lord Hazelton stopped when his gaze fell on something across the Serpentine, between sections of trees that had been planted to provide the feeling of a wood. Caro's brow dropped to a frown, and she turned to see what had his attention.

Her heart dropped to her stomach a moment later at the sight of Miss Dobson sneaking out from behind a cluster of trees and dashing a few yards toward the path...where Mr. Newman was approaching her.

"You must excuse me, my darling," Lord Hazelton said in a suddenly distracted voice, backing away from her. "The friends I was set to meet appear to have arrived. But fear not, this will only take a moment." He wiggled his brow, then turned to dash off toward the end of the Serpentine.

Caro gaped at him and at Miss Dobson and Mr. Newman, who had just reached each other and began speaking rapidly. She was still gaping when Rufus charged up to her.

"What did he say?" he demanded. "How did he offend you? I'll tear the man limb from limb with my bare hands."

Caro silenced him by grasping his arm and nodding across the water. "Look," she whispered. "They're going to try to sell the diamond again. Right now."

CHAPTER 7

*C*aro's statement was so far from what Rufus expected to hear that it took a moment for the full impact of her words to sink in. He gaped at her for a moment before she repeated, "Miss Dobson. Mr. Newman. And Lord Hazelton is here to meet with them."

Rufus's nerves went taut, and he whipped around to assess the situation for himself. Sure enough, Miss Dobson and Newman stood close together on the far side of the Serpentine. Hazelton was still in the process of rounding the end of the water, but he was clearly heading toward them.

"Are they mad?" Rufus exclaimed. "It's the middle of the day. The park is crowded. We can see them and they can see us."

"I am not entirely certain that they have seen us,

though," Caro said, grabbing his arm and fast-walking him along the path in the same way Hazelton had gone.

"Are you suggesting we confront them?" Rufus asked incredulously, rushing along with Caro all the same.

"Perhaps," Caro said.

Her answer was as mad as the meeting that was about to take place. The trouble was, Rufus wanted to see an end to the mystery surrounding the diamond theft and for the guilty parties to be brought to justice more than he needed the world around him to make sense. He charged ahead with Caro, heedless of the people who stopped to stare at them as they broke every rule of propriety.

They steered clear of Lady Malvis in their quest, but Rufus honestly wasn't certain his intended fiancée would have noticed one way or another. Two of Caro's most cunning students and friends had flanked her and were steering her toward a row of benches that looked out on the winter-withered rose garden.

"They are simply the most magnificent books imaginable," the dark-haired one was saying. "Every woman in London is devouring them."

"Yes," the lighter-haired one agreed. "They're ever so naughty."

"If they are naughty, I want nothing to do with them," Lady Malvis said, attempting to extract herself from the ladies. She glanced around, presumably searching for Rufus, but Caro's friends forced her to pay attention to them.

"Here," the dark-haired one said. "Let's sit here and we'll read aloud to you."

"I'm not sure—" Lady Malvis started, but for a change, she was helpless and speechless. Caro's friends wedged her onto a bench as though they were jailers set to guard a dangerous prisoner.

"Remind me to thank Felicity and Eliza profusely later," Caro said in a distracted rush as she skipped around the side of the Serpentine, Rufus in tow.

"If they can keep her distracted for the next twenty years, I'll reward them with their own kingdoms," Rufus said with a shake of his head.

"Just promise me one thing," Caro said as they reached the far side of the water. She seemed to have deliberately positioned the two of them so that one of the stands of trees blocked their view to where Miss Dobson, Newman, and Hazelton presumably stood.

"Anything," Rufus said, meaning it from the bottom of his heart. "I'll promise you anything."

Caro glanced over her shoulder to him with a grin that radiated mischief. "Promise me you haven't proposed to her yet."

"I haven't," Rufus said proudly.

"And promise me that you won't," Caro went on. "At least, not today."

"My father will have my hide if I—"

"Promise me," Caro insisted. "And trust me."

It would have been pointless of him to attempt resistance. "I promise," he said.

Her smile widened for a moment before she grew serious once more. They reached the stand of trees, but rather than edge around it to come close enough to over-hear whatever conversation was happening between Miss Dobson, Newman, and Hazelton, Caro charged right into it.

"What in the devil's name," Rufus began, but thought better of making any noise.

The trees had been planted to resemble a patch of woodland, and they did their job effectively. The light dimmed and the temperature dropped as the pine boughs blocked the sky above. There were a good number of shrubs planted between the trees, giving the space the feeling of a thicket. Rufus wondered how many other couples had availed themselves of the unexpectedly private spot right in the middle of the very public park. He wondered how many other thieves and cutpurses had made the densely-packed shrubbery their den as well. It was something of a surprise that they hadn't bowled right into a pack of thieving urchins plotting their next heist.

Those thoughts flew right out of his head as they reached the far edge of the trees. Caro motioned for him to be silent and to crouch so that they wouldn't be seen behind a particularly thick and particularly sharp holly bush. The barbs of the holly were worth it, in the end. Miss Dobson, Newman, and Hazelton had latched on to a similar idea to Caro's and stood close to the edge of the woods for concealment.

"—and I won't take no for an answer," Hazelton was

in the midst of saying. "Not this time. Not when I have a nubile, young bride to impress."

Caro made a retching sound that was almost loud enough to give them away. Rufus reached for her hand and squeezed it to steady her.

"It's become too dangerous," Newman said. "They're on to us, the lot of them."

"Lord Herrington and that whore of a—I mean, your fiancée, Lord Hazelton, if you please, barged into my father's home just yesterday to demand I surrender the diamond and all who have touched it," Miss Dobson said.

Rufus arched an eyebrow at the twisted explanation of what had happened in Kent.

"Which is why the sale must take place swiftly," Hazelton said. "I'd've brought you the blunt this afternoon if you'd let me."

"I couldn't have sold you the diamond here if I'd wanted to," Newman said, sending a thrill of victory through Rufus—the man had confessed to the theft, he'd heard it with his own ears—only to crash a moment later. "I don't have the diamond in my possession."

"What?" Miss Dobson gasped. "You said you did. You said you had it and were ready to sell it. You said you'd give me ten percent of the sale for finding you a buyer."

"Keep your voice down, woman," Newman snapped at her.

Caro tensed, radiating anger. Rufus squeezed her hand to remind her silence was of the essence.

"I do not have the diamond in my possession," Newman went on, "because it never left the East India Company's house."

"What?" Miss Dobson gasped, voicing the same shock that Rufus felt to the tips of his toes.

"The diamond is still within Khan's house," Newman repeated.

"Khan," Caro whispered, barely audible. "Saif Khan. I knew he was involved somehow. He must be holding it for Newman."

"But if the diamond was never stolen to begin with, how can you sell it to me?" Hazelton asked, baffled and blustering.

"I never said it wasn't stolen," Newman muttered, "just that it never left the house."

"Please explain, sir," Hazelton said gruffly, crossing his arms.

Newman huffed out a breath and rubbed a hand over his face. "Khan was supposed to present it as a gift to the king's representative," he explained. "The house was crawling with men. Removing it would have meant certain discovery. So instead, I nicked it from its case about an hour before the presentation and relocated it to another object in the house."

"Relocated it?" Miss Dobson asked incredulously, clasping a hand to her chest.

"I came up with the idea of stuffing it up your cunny a little too late, love," Newman said with a sly drawl.

"I knew it," Caro whispered, turning to Rufus.

"That's what Rebecca heard him say when she was watching the two of them—"

Rufus touched a finger to his lips to silence her.

"Why do you think I keep bloody risking my neck to go back for Khan's bloody revels?" Newman went on, growing more upset by the moment. "I've tried a dozen times and more to retrieve the diamond, but they keep moving the—" his expression grew suddenly cagey, "—the thing I put it in."

"What did you put it in?" Hazelton asked like the buffoon he was.

Newman's face lit as though the sun had come up. "You bring me the money I asked for and I'll tell you where it's hidden. You can retrieve it yourself."

"That's a might risky, don't you think?" Hazelton argued.

Newman shrugged. "You want the diamond, I'll tell you where to get it."

Hazelton growled but said nothing further.

"Khan is having another of his routs tomorrow night," Newman went on. "You bring me the cash and I'll tell you where it is. I'll even help create a distraction so that you can pop it out and tuck it away in your pocket when no one is looking. Hell, you can stick it up Henny here's honey pot and let her walk out with it between her legs, if you'd like."

Hazelton made a sound as though he were tempted and turned to Miss Dobson, wiggling his eyebrows in that odious way of his. For her part, Miss Dobson eyed the old goat up and down as though considering it.

"Do we have a deal, then?" Newman asked, extending a hand to Hazelton.

Hazelton hesitated for only a moment, glancing to Miss Dobson once, then reached out and shook Newman's hand. "We have a deal. Tomorrow night it is, then."

"Fine." Newman nodded. "Now be off with you. We've garnered too much notice already."

That was it. None of the three of them said goodbye or loitered where they were. They peeled off in different directions, evidently trying to get as far away from each other as possible.

Caro shifted to face Rufus, standing and taking both of his hands. "That was everything we could have hoped for and more," she said, her eyes shining. "Except one thing."

"Saif Khan," Rufus said, reading the answer in her eyes. "I know the man is bloody well involved. He has to know where the diamond is hiding within his father's house. He has to be involved in some way."

"He is involved," a serious, male voice said just feet away from them.

Caro gasped and leapt toward Rufus, and Rufus's blood ran cold as Saif himself emerged from the shadows of the shrubs. He was dressed completely in black and held a dully gleaming pistol in one hand. The second he noticed it, Rufus stepped in front of Caro, blocking her completely from Saif's treachery.

"You hurt her and I swear, Saif, I'll end your miserable days on this earth with my bare hands," he said in a threatening voice.

Saif's stance shifted and he held his hands up—one of them still holding the pistol, which Rufus noticed was not cocked—in an appeasing gesture. "I would never dream of hurting a woman of such beauty and cleverness," he said.

Rufus frowned, the hair on the back of his neck standing up. Something wasn't right. "What are you doing here?" he demanded. "Come to make certain your cronies carry out your deal?"

Saif frowned. "My deal?" He glanced to Caro as she stepped to Rufus's side and glared at Saif. "Is it true that the two of you pursued Miss Dobson to her father's country house yesterday?"

"We did," Caro answered, tilting up her head.

Saif narrowed his eyes. "Why would you do that? Why not tell the Runners her whereabouts instead?"

"The Runners believe me to be a suspect in the theft," Rufus said. "Had we told them, they would have accused me of collusion."

"No, we wouldn't," Saif told him.

Rufus opened his mouth to argue, but the meaning of Saif's statement struck him like a stone between the eyes. He continued to gape for a moment before saying, "I beg your pardon?"

"We know you're not the thief," Saif said. "We've been certain you and Felix are innocent for several weeks now."

It was Caro's turn to stare at Saif in open-mouth wonder. "Do you mean to say that you are a Bow Street Runner, sir?" she asked, her eyes going wide.

Saif treated her to a saucy grin and touched his forehead in a salute. "At your service, my lady."

"No," Rufus hissed incredulously. "You?"

Saif nodded. "Indeed."

"Saif Khan?" Rufus continued, shaking his head. "Bounder, drunk, ladies' man?"

"All an act, my friend." Saif stepped forward enough to thump Rufus's arm. "I was recruited direct from university. Gibbon thought it would be useful to have a colonial on staff. Nobs hereabouts tend to underestimate us." He glanced to Caro with a wink.

"You mean to tell me that you're not a spoiled Casanova?" Rufus still couldn't comprehend it.

"Well," Saif said with a modest shrug, "I do enjoy the company of ladies of all sorts."

"It was you." Caro narrowed her eyes and leaned threateningly toward him. "In the secret passageway the other night. That is to say, we assumed it was you, but it truly was."

"I confess it was," Saif said, looking suddenly sheepish. He glanced to Rufus. "I may need to have you tutor me in the art of making a woman squeal the way you did. I believe you know the effect it had on me. It was all I could do to make myself scarce after my unfortunate lapse of concentration."

A flash of fury soured Rufus's stomach, though he had to admit that Caro constituted a serious lapse of concentration for him as well in a great many ways.

Saif broke the awkward silence that followed with, "We have much to thank the two of you for. Try as we did, none of us could discover Miss Dobson's whereabouts."

"Did you try asking a woman?" Caro asked, one eyebrow arched.

Saif could only answer with a guilty look. "We've known Newman is the thief for weeks now, we just haven't had any way of proving it. And now we know why."

"You do?" Rufus asked, as irritated as Caro looked.

"The diamond was never removed from my father's house," Saif said. "We've been breaking our backs for weeks trying to figure out how we could raid Newman's lodgings to find it. As it is, it may be difficult to prove it was stolen at all if it remains under my father's roof."

"Newman could claim it was moved or misplaced by a servant and that he knew nothing about it," Rufus said, the pieces coming together in his mind.

"But not anymore," Saif said. "Now we have witnesses to his confession—the two of you."

"But he could still get away with everything," Caro said, dropping her arms. "We merely heard him say the diamond is still in the house. He never said where it was. He could still claim he knows nothing about it."

"Which is why we need the prospective sale to continue," Saif went on. "At least until the very last moment. We need to catch them all in the act or we have nothing."

"Not even the diamond," Caro said. "It could be anywhere."

"Precisely," Saif said.

Another, ruminating silence fell. The situation seemed so close to being resolved and yet still so far out of reach. But at least Rufus now understood why Saif had suddenly appeared in the room at the same time as Newman, Miss Dobson, and Hazelton the night Felix and Jo thought they'd caught the thief. He'd sprung onto the scene in order to catch them in the act himself.

"You thought Felix was involved," he said aloud as more pieces came together. "The night the diamond was almost sold before."

"What other reason would he and Miss Hodges have had to be there?" Saif asked, confirming his suspicions.

"Then why did you run from them?" Caro asked.

Saif frowned. "At the time, they were believed to be criminals. I feared for my life after revealing myself."

Rufus narrowed his eyes. "Felix would never harm a hair on your head. After all our years of friendship, how could you distrust either of us so much?"

Saif lowered his head, then shrugged. "My only

defense is that one learns to trust no one when delicate matters of investigation are at stake. And I could ask the same of you. We've known each other since university, and yet you would suspect me of stealing from my own father?"

Rufus's face went hot and his skin suddenly seemed too tight. He rolled his shoulders to dispel the awkward sensation, but it was no good. "I'm sorry, old friend," he said. "Allow me to make it up to you by offering my help in any way that you might find useful to bring this matter to a close."

"Apology accepted," Saif said, offering his hand. The two shook, and while their hands were still clasped, Saif said, "I could use your help, you know." He glanced to Caro. "I know that you and your friends are well-acquainted with the secret passages in my father's house. Father wishes to keep them as closely-guarded a secret as possible. If you are willing to participate in what I'm certain will be a final operation to catch Newman and his accomplices in the act, then fewer people would need to be made aware of the passages."

"We'll help in any way we can," Caro said. "Just tell us how." She glanced to Rufus for confirmation.

Rufus nodded to her, a new sense of purpose filling him. If Caro played an instrumental role in defeating a notorious diamond thief, then perhaps his father would see clear to allowing him to marry her instead of Lady Malvis. It was the last hope he had for ensuring the only thing that could make him happy for the rest of his life.

CHAPTER 8

*I*t was unusual for Caro not to feel in control of any given situation, but as the day of what she was coming to call The Final Party in her mind wore on, her nerves bristled. Rufus was late. He should have been there hours ago to plan their evening's course. It was a bad sign that she hadn't heard so much as a peep from him all day.

"This will be fantastic," Felicity told both her and Eliza as the three of them dressed in the room that had formerly been Miss Dobson's bedchamber. It was the largest bedchamber in the house, and the two wily young ladies had commandeered it as soon as Miss Dobson was gone. "An entire house filled with sin."

"I simply do not know how I will be able to maintain my focus with so many handsome men about," Eliza agreed, pinning Felicity's curls into a fetching style atop her head.

Caro sent the two a warning look as she paced the far end of the room, already dressed in one of her more revealing gowns. "I'm afraid you may encounter more than you realize," she told them. "The bacchanals our neighbors throw are of the most scandalous variety. You may find yourselves manhandled in shocking ways."

"Yes, please," Eliza said in a longing voice, winking at Felicity in the mirror.

The two of them shared a flurry of giggles that did little to set Caro's mind at ease. Of all the young ladies at the school, Felicity and Eliza were by far the cleverest. She needed them to be alert and to think quickly in the mission they were all undertaking. If Mr. Newman caught so much as a hint that his game was up, he might bolt yet again. Which was why, as much as Caro might have wanted them there, Rebecca, Nigel, Jo, and Felix couldn't attend. They would certainly be standing by outside of the East India Company's house, but one sight of them and the guilty parties would know trouble was afoot. If it wasn't for the fact that she and Rufus had become a regular part of Khan's parties, they might not have been able to attend either.

Where was Rufus? The party was racing toward them and he still hadn't arrived.

"There's no need to be so anxious," Felicity told her when Eliza finished with her hair and the two of them switched places. "The plan is in place. You know that Mr. Newman, Miss Dobson, and Lord Hazelton will be in attendance tonight and that they will, out of necessity, attempt to carry out their dastardly plans."

"And you have all of us in league with you," Eliza added as Felicity drew a brush through her hair. "What could possibly go wrong?"

Everything, Caro answered for herself. "You are right," she said aloud, pressing a hand over her stomach to quell the butterflies that rose up at her lie. "I should check on the Runners," she added, turning and fleeing from the room.

The rest of the school was more of a reflection of her inner turmoil than the confidence Felicity and Eliza exhibited, for in the last eight hours, the school had transformed. It was no longer simply a disreputable holding pen for wayward young ladies, it was a staging ground for what an outside observer would have viewed as the largest operation the Bow Street Runners had ever undertaken.

"Oh, my lady," Flora rushed up to Caro as she descended the stairs to the chaotic ground floor. She could already hear the chatter of half a dozen young ladies and twice as many men coming from the dining room.

"Has Lord Herrington arrived yet?" Caro asked before Flora could say whatever was clearly worrying her.

"No, my lady," Flora said. "But the Runners are more than enough. They'll eat us out of house and home, they will."

"The Runners need to be well-fed before we begin our evening's task," Caro said with a sigh. Though she suspected it would take a great deal of money and careful purchasing to restock the school's larders.

"Yes, my lady," Flora said, still distressed. She continued to follow Caro as she headed toward the dining room, adding, "I fear more than a few of the girls will lose their virtue tonight if they're not careful."

As soon as Caro turned the corner into the dining room, she saw exactly what Flora meant. At least a dozen Runners were seated at the long tables on either side of the dining room. Most were dressed in plain clothes and would be standing ready outside the East India Company's house during the party until they were called upon. A few were dressed elaborately enough to attend the party, though, including Mr. Gibbon, the man Nigel had introduced as his superior. The Runners were gobbling up what looked like a small feast spread across the tables and trying to pay attention as Mr. Gibbon marched up and down the aisles between the tables reminding his men of their assignments.

But the young ladies of the school were making his task hard. Caro paused inside the doorway to the room, her eyes going wide. It was as though none of the ladies had ever seen a man before. Some of her young friends sat on the benches beside the Runners, gazing adoringly up at them as they ate or stroking their arms to feel their muscles. A few had engaged some of the gentlemen in lively conversation, which happened to involve running their fingers through the gentlemen's hair or tracing the outline of their ears. In the far corner of the room, one of the girls sat astride a Runner's lap, their mouths merged in a shocking kiss. Judging by the way the Runner's hands moved to bunch up the young lady's skirts, Flora was dead right about the possibility of virtue being imminently lost.

"Stop that," Mr. Gibbon shouted, noticing the amorous couple just as Caro did. "Pull yourself together, man."

He marched down one side of the room as Caro tore down the other. They reached the couple just as the Runner came to his senses and lifted the young lady off his lap. Caro nearly laughed to discover the lady to be none other than Miss Warren, the only one of Miss Dobson's favorites who had stayed at the school.

"Really, Miss Warren?" Caro asked, trying her best not to laugh at the absurdity of it all.

Miss Warren glared at her. "You shouldn't be the only one to enjoy yourself. If we're all damned, we might as well be damned with pleasure."

Caro raised an eyebrow, not at Miss Warren's sass, but because she had a fair point. The young lady didn't stay around to discuss it, however. She stomped off, her head held high.

"Perhaps it wasn't such a good idea to stage our operations from the school," Mr. Gibbon said.

Caro turned to agree with him to find that he was speaking to Nigel Kent, not her.

"It's a damn sight better than staging operations from the square," Nigel replied. "Begging your pardon, Lady Caroline," he said with an apologetic bow for his language.

He could have sworn like a sailor at her for all Caro was concerned. If Nigel was there, it meant Rebecca was as well. She left the gentlemen to their planning and twisted to search the room for Rebecca.

The moment she spotted Rebecca—and Jo as well—standing in the doorway, looking flabbergasted at the pandemonium that reigned in the room, Caro picked up her skirts and ran to greet them.

"I have never been gladder to see friends in all my life," she said with emotion from the bottom of her heart, hugging Rebecca and Jo in turn.

"Tonight we catch the diamond thief," Rebecca said excitedly. "We would not have missed this for anything."

"Certainly not," Jo agreed, squeezing Caro's hand. "I am only sad that we cannot show ourselves at the party."

"But we will be watching from the secret passageway," Rebecca whispered, glancing around. "Nigel says we're not to breathe a word about that to anyone, not even Mr. Gibbon, though."

"Saif Khan doesn't want anyone more than necessary knowing about the passages," Caro agreed in a whisper, gesturing for her friends to walk with her into the hall where they could speak more freely.

"I still cannot believe Saif Khan is a Runner," Jo said.

"That is to say, we saw him engaged in—" she swallowed, "—activity."

"Even Runners have needs," Caro said, then shook her head. She had no interest in discussing Saif Khan's proclivities when so much was about to happen. "We will only have a limited amount of time tonight. If Mr. Newman catches wind that—"

She stopped as the front door opened and Rufus stepped through. Caro could see in an instant something was wrong. He should have been excited, but a dark sort of melancholy hung over him like a raincloud. It could only mean one thing.

She flew down the hall to meet him, but instead of flinging herself into his arms as she wanted to, she stopped just in front of him, her whole body vibrating with dread, and asked, "Did you propose to Lady Malvis?"

"No," Rufus said, his shoulders dropping.

Relief like nothing Caro had ever felt washed through her, even though she could tell there was more to the story. She grabbed Rufus's hand and led him into the nearest classroom, shutting the door. "Tell me what happened," she demanded.

Rufus pushed a hand through his hair, causing it to stand up awkwardly, and blew out a breath. "Father was not pleased when I returned home yesterday without proposing," he said, the look in his eyes telling Caro he was understating the matter. "We rowed fiercely. And we rowed again just now, before he allowed me to leave the house."

"You're a grown man," Caro said, crossing her arms with a scowl. "He has no right to confine you to the house."

Rufus let out a wry laugh. "Tell that to Father." He shook his head. "I explained everything to him, and I mean everything, about the two of us."

Caro gulped before she could steady herself. "And what did he say?" she asked, her voice hoarse.

Rufus shrugged. "He said the same as he said the other day, when he saw you in the carriage. He was sorry, but the family comes first."

Caro's gut burned hot with the injustice of it all.

"He does understand, I think," Rufus went on, stepping forward to take her hands. "The man is not made of stone. He said he would look the other way and direct others to do so as well if we wish to continue our relationship."

"How magnanimous of him," Caro grumbled, her jaw tense. Although she had to admit that there was a fair degree of generosity in Lord Herrington's stance. The simple fact that men had kept women outside of their marriages since the dawn of time did not mean that the practice was spoken of or approved of in polite society. It was quite liberal of Rufus's father to acknowledge love in the face of duty.

"Even if he had sworn to disown me for keeping you," Rufus said, pulling her into his embrace, "I would have told him to go to hell. I may be doomed to do my duty for my family, but I love you, Caro. More than I will ever love any woman."

"And I love you," Caro said, her heart melting even as it threatened to break. She brushed her hand over the side of his face. "More than you can know."

"Say you'll be mine in whatever way is possible for us," he went on. "Say you'll be my mistress, my one true love. Let me love you, adore you, and fill you with babies on a regular basis, or at least try to." The spark of mischief was back in his eyes.

Seeing that spark in him reignited it in her. "Is that what you want?" she asked, one eyebrow raised. "A garden of babies."

"With my red hair and your cleverness," he said, then tugged her close and kissed her hard.

Caro's confidence returned inch by liquid inch as their kiss deepened. The fire in her belly roared to life once more, heating her and sending the delicious ache she loved so much pulsing through her sex. That feeling of arousal increased as he scooped a hand into her low-cut bodice to fondle her breast and bring her nipple to hardness in a gesture that had become so familiar to her. It reminded her of her plans, of the work she had been so tirelessly engaged in to ensure that the two of them could be together. It would all come to fruition tonight. All she had to do was keep her wits about her and remember the true goal of the evening.

"You're not married yet," she reminded him, panting,

as they broke apart. "And you won't ever be married to Lady Malvis if I have anything to do with it."

"But, darling, her wealth—"

Caro shook her head and pressed a finger to his kiss-swollen lips. "As you said, I'm clever." Her grin grew as the fire of determination burned hotly inside of her once more. "Clever young ladies get what they want, one way or another. Never doubt for a moment that I want you, or that I can have you."

He studied her with glittering fire in his eyes. "If you can produce a miracle of love, I will never doubt anything you say for the rest of our lives."

A knock sounded at the door, interrupting the beauty of the moment.

"You're needed in the dining room," Nigel's voice sounded from the hall.

"We'll be there directly," Rufus answered. He met Caro's eyes once more. "So much is at stake tonight."

"We will not fail," Caro told him.

That determination stayed with her as the two of them left the classroom and went to join the others. The dining room had been restored to a semblance of order, although the young ladies of the school still sat interspersed with the Runners and most continued to gaze at their companions in adoration. Felicity and Eliza had come down from their preparations and stood with Rebecca and Jo just inside the dining room door, along with Nigel and Felix. Caro and Rufus joined them.

"This will be a delicate operation," Mr. Gibbon said

from the front of the room, "and speed is of the essence. We know that the Chandramukhi Diamond is still somewhere within the East India Company's house. We know that Wallace Newman will try to sell it to Lord Hazelton tonight and that Miss Henrietta Dobson may be an accomplice in that sale. It is imperative that we catch all three of them in the act so that they can be arrested and charged."

He shifted his stance to look at the rows of Runners still finishing up their supper. "Men, I want you stationed outside the house, monitoring everyone who comes in and, more importantly, who goes out. If anyone leaves under suspicious circumstances, I want you to tail them until you are convinced of their innocence."

He stood taller and glanced to the back of the room, where Caro and Rufus and the others stood. "Those of you who will attend the party, keep your eyes open, but blend in. We need to track every move our suspects make, but we need to find that diamond as well. Khan is aware of what we are up to. Saif will coordinate with him." He nodded to Saif, who stood at the edge of Caro's group of friends. Saif nodded in return.

"Ladies," Mr. Gibbon addressed the young ladies of the school last of all. "There is a fair chance that Miss Dobson may try to hide in the school or make her presence known here in some way if her part of tonight's deal goes awry. I am relying on you to catch her and keep her here if that is the case."

"Yes, sir," one of the young ladies answered from the front. "We'll do anything for you."

"Yes, we will." Her statement echoed around the room.

Mr. Gibbon turned a deep shade of red and cleared his throat, as though the young ladies had offered something else entirely. He glanced to Nigel at the back of the room with a hint of desperation, then squared his shoulders and nodded.

"Good," he said at last. "Let's be about our business, then."

CHAPTER 9

*R*ufus had promised to believe Caro and to trust her in all things, but as they made their way around the crowded, noisy ballroom in the East India Company's house, he was convinced that some things were very much easier said than done.

"Lord Herrington, may I offer my heartfelt congratulations," an inebriated Lord Whitlock said as he leapt away from his companions to stop Rufus and Caro.

Rufus liked Whitlock. He'd spent many a raucous evening in the dark-haired young viscount's company, but with so much on the line, he didn't have time to play any of Whitlock's games.

"Congratulations for what, sir?" he asked, attempting to shield Caro when Whitlock's hazy-eyed gaze fell heavily on her mostly-exposed breasts.

"On your new leg shackle," Whitlock said, righting

himself enough to slap Rufus's back. "I hear Lady Malvis is a valuable catch."

Rufus's nerves bristled. "It's not a done deal yet," he said, prying himself away from Whitlock once more.

"But you're in the same boat as the rest of us, no?" Whitlock asked.

"Boat, sir?"

"You're manning the rigging along with the rest of us who are forced to marry for means. It's perfectly understandable." Whitlock managed to pull himself straight enough almost to look sober. "It'll be my turn at the gallows next."

"You can have Lady Malvis," Rufus said in as joking a tone as he could manage. He was already scanning the room, searching for a spot where he and Caro could stand to spot Newman and Hazelton the moment either arrived.

"Truly?" Whitlock asked, looking as though he would consider it. "She's quite a prize. But perhaps you think you've got a better prize?" He smiled groggily at Caro, or rather, her breasts.

"Lord Herrington will end up with a prize that no one expects," Caro said, hooking her arm through Rufus's and dragging him deeper into the room.

Rufus would have brushed the encounter off, except that he received three other hearty rounds of congratulations before making it to the side of the dais where the musicians were seated.

"Are you certain you didn't propose to Lady Malvis

and then forget you did?" Caro asked with a grin that hid a more anxious twist of emotion in her eyes.

"I swear on my life, I didn't," he said with a frown. "But something must have been said somewhere.

"Ask a woman," Caro laughed, though it was clear the laughter was for show, as was the way she pressed her body against him and began to fiddle with the buttons of his jacket. "Women always know the business of other women, particularly when it comes to new engagements."

She had a firm point. Although from the moment she wrapped her arms around his neck, Rufus would much rather have given his full attention to her. It was laughable how a flirtation that had begun as a way to observe a room full of suspicious people could shift into something so vital to his soul so quickly. A few seconds of inattention wouldn't compromise their mission too desperately, or so he told himself as he slanted his mouth over Caro's, kissing her with the full strength of the passion that bloomed in his heart.

Caro melted against him, her body fitting with his in all the right places. Her mouth was supple and needy, and she kissed him back with as much ardor as he felt. If it were not for the four dozen or so other people in the room, he would have taken her up against the wall in time to the rhythm of the lively dance the orchestra played.

As soon as that delicious thought entered his head, a slap on his back jerked him back to reality and away from

Caro. He turned to glare at whoever had disturbed their passion only to find Saif grinning at him.

"You of all people cannot afford distractions, friend," Saif said, his eyes deadly serious in spite of his jovial expression.

"I was about to tell him the same thing," Caro said in an overly cheerful voice, though her eyes also told a different story.

"I know what I'm about," Rufus insisted.

Saif's expression softened to sympathy. "Bad luck about the engagement, my friend."

"There is no engagement," Rufus told him, more frustrated than ever. "Where is this rumor coming from?"

"Father heard from Lord Shackleford that Lady Shackleford called on Lady Malvis herself this morning. Apparently your lovely fiancée-to-be was supposed to receive her proposal yesterday, but when she didn't, she asked her friends to put it about that the deal was done. As a way to speed you along, no doubt."

"No doubt," Rufus growled, on the verge of throwing a fist through the nearest wall.

Saif slapped his back once more in what might have been an attempt to calm him. "It's a shame you weren't able to recover the diamond on your own."

"What? Why?" Rufus snapped.

Saif shrugged. "Father is offering a tremendous reward for its safe return," he said. "Everyone has been talking about it. Imagine all the things you could do if you found the diamond before the Runners do or before Newman and Hazelton make their move."

The devilishness in Saif's eyes sent an eerie chill through Rufus. Saif was a Runner. He owed his allegiance to the crown. He couldn't possibly be suggesting that there might be profit in beating the Runners to the punch.

"I know who my father would rather give the reward money to," Saif said, then stepped away. "Newman's carriage was just spotted in the line to drop guests at the house for the night," he said, then winked and marched off into the swirling crowd of dancers, sweeping a woman in a sopping wet dress into his arms.

"Did he just suggest what I believe he did?" Caro asked in awe.

Rufus turned to her. "That if we can find the diamond before Newman completes his sale with Hazelton, we might secure the reward money?"

Caro flushed a shade of pink that was so alluring that under any other circumstances Rufus would have whisked her immediately off to a private room to have his way with her. "Oh, but this is brilliant," she said, beaming. "Between the reward money and—" She snapped her lips shut, her grin even more impish. "I am quite certain it would be more than enough."

Rufus took her hand. "We'd better hurry our search, then."

. . .

Caro's heart beat so hard as she ducked and dodged through dancing, laughing, flirting couples in the ballroom that she was certain her breasts would pop right out of her bodice due to the force.

"I wish we had more time to think about where the diamond is hidden," she said breathlessly over her shoulder to Rufus. "It's a shame the house is so large."

"And filled with so many places to hide," Rufus answered.

He was right. The entire house had been designed and arranged for assignations and clandestine meetings. There were a thousand places and more to hide a diamond.

"We should start by looking in the room where Rebecca first saw Mr. Newman with Miss Dobson," she said as they neared the doorway. "And any other room where Mr. Newman is known to have been in the last two months."

"That could be anywhere," Rufus said. "The upstairs room, the room where the exchange nearly happened, the refreshment room, here."

Caro opened her mouth to weigh in on his list, but she was stopped as none other than the Duchess of Cavendish stepped into her path.

"My dear Lady Caroline," the intimidating, older woman said, a knowing grin lighting her expression. "May I be the first to congratulate you on your most recent triumph?"

Caro and Rufus were forced to stop in their tracks.

One did not dismiss a duchess in order to search for a diamond.

"My triumph, my lady?" Caro asked, dropping into a short, awkward curtsy as protocol dictated. She glanced to Rufus, wondering if Lady Malvis's rumor had somehow twisted its way into people believing she was the one to whom Rufus had become engaged.

But no, the duchess laughed and said, "Perhaps I should refer to it as Mrs. Vickers's triumph?"

Caro's heart dropped into her dancing shoes. The duchess looked entirely too pleased with herself for Caro to stop what she feared the fine lady would say next. Worse still, a pair of younger ladies who appeared to be accompanying her at the night's festivities turned away from the flirtations they had begun to listen in on the conversation.

"Oh," Caro stammered, scrambling for some way to break through the wall of admirers who looked ready to pounce. "I could hardly take credit for something so grand, your grace."

She sent a sideways look to Rufus. Perhaps fortunately, he looked more confused than anything else. If there was a way she could rush on without the duchess saying more....

"And you must be the inspiration for our dear Mrs. Vickers's books," the duchess said, turning to Rufus with a saucy wink.

"I beg your pardon?" Rufus said, genuinely baffled.

"Mrs. Vickers," the duchess said, blinking rapidly. "Surely, you must know who Mrs. Vickers is."

Rufus looked more confused than ever, but said, "She is the authoress of the books that have become so popular of late, is she not?"

The duchess laughed, and her companions laughed with her. "How very droll of you. Lady Caroline is Mrs. Vickers," she said as though explaining to a child that the sky was filled with clouds.

Puzzlement lingered for a few more moments in Rufus's expression until, all at once, he understood. The moment the truth came to him, his brow shot up to his hairline and shock lit his green eyes. He turned to Caro with a quickly-spreading grin.

"No," he said, shocked and amused at once.

"A lady never spills her secrets," Caro answered, her smile coy.

"A wise answer, Lady Caroline," the duchess said with an approving nod.

"Thank you, your grace," Caro said, bobbing another curtsy.

She stood and was about to say more when, past the duchess's shoulder, she spotted the portly figure of Lord Hazelton arriving in the front hall. With a gasp, she reached back and grabbed Rufus's hand, praying he would see what she saw without her having to bring further attention to Lord Hazelton or to herself.

Rufus's hand closed around hers, and he took a small step forward. "If you will excuse me, your grace," he said with a gracious nod for the duchess. "Now that I have discovered Mrs. Vickers's identity, I believe I have a few suggestions to impart for her next publication."

Blessedly, the duchess and her friends burst into tittering laughter. "By all means, Lord Herrington. I have been informed that parties hosted by Mr. Khan are designed for such assignations."

In other circumstances, Caro might have been embarrassed by the duchess's overt statement. As it was, the clock in her brain was ticking. She curtsied one more time and blurted some sort of nicety that was forgotten the moment Rufus slipped an arm around her waist and whisked her out into the hall.

"Mrs. Vickers?" he asked in a low voice as they rushed away from the ballroom and the front door—where Lord Hazelton appeared not to have noticed them yet—and as far away as they could get.

"There isn't time," Caro whispered in return, taking the lead and rushing ahead of him.

In a trice, she realized the error of the direction they'd taken in their flight from the front of the house.

"We won't be able to search upstairs," she said, stumbling to a halt at the end of the hall. "Not without risking Lord Hazelton noticing us as we make our way to the stairs."

"Perhaps we could use the servant's stairs?" Rufus suggested. "Or the secret passageway," he added in a hush, even though no one was around them.

Caro chewed on her lip. "We could use the secret passageway. There is an entrance through here."

She took his hand and marched into the closest room, closing the door behind them.

"Hold on," Rufus said, tugging her to a stop halfway across the room to where she thought the hidden door was located. Caro stopped, and when she glanced to Rufus in question, he said, "This is the room where they nearly sold the diamond before."

"It is," Caro agreed with a nod.

Rufus shrugged. "Why not begin our search here?"

Caro glanced around, her heart sinking. The room was massive. Not only that, it contained several cabinets, tables, chairs, and sofas. There was a narrow table along one wall that held several carved boxes and a golden statue of the Hindu god Ganesh with a large ruby in his forehead. Beyond that, the ornate wallpaper could have concealed any number of doors or secret nooks. A giant, oriental carpet might have covered any number of trap-doors. The tall windows along one side of the room were hung with thick curtains which could have had secret pockets sewn into them.

"It will take hours to search this room alone," Caro said, letting out a disappointed breath. Perhaps Saif Khan hadn't done them much of a favor after all.

"True," Rufus agreed, looking far more enthusiastic than she felt. "But we must start somewhere."

"If you say so," she said, giving his hand a squeeze.

When she let go, they split apart, each moving to

opposite sides of the room to search for the diamond. Caro moved toward the fireplace, running her hands along the sides and the mantel to feel for any sort of latch or hidden compartment. Five minutes of searching brought nothing. She even took one of the fire irons and poked around the hot bricks in back of the fire.

"It's not here," she called softly across the room to Rufus.

"It doesn't appear to be in this cabinet either," Rufus said, shutting the cabinet he'd been searching.

Caro moved on to check a second cabinet beside the fireplace while Rufus began pulling out small drawers that were set in an elaborate writing desk in the corner. The second cabinet had just as many tiny drawers, but all Caro found were papers, quills, packets of ink, seals, and a large variety of other items that were decidedly not diamonds.

"It's not in the desk," Rufus called from across the room.

"Nor is it in his cabinet," Caro said, her frustration showing in her voice.

"Is it worth checking the furnishings for concealed pockets?" Rufus asked as he moved to the largest sofa in the room.

"I don't see why not," Caro said with a sigh.

She tried to bolster her enthusiasm by moving to the table with the statue of Ganesh. There was something both fascinating and soothing about the elephant-headed god, and she could use a deity to help in her search. It seemed far too obvious for the diamond to be hidden in any of the carved boxes on the table, but she checked each one all the same.

She was about to move on when an irregularity in the wallpaper behind the statue caught her eye. It looked to her like one of the latches that opened the doors to the secret passageway. Could it be a secret compartment in the wall? Hope soared as she leaned closer to get a look at it. She bit her lip, and when she was convinced it might be something, she grabbed Ganesh to move him to the side.

Her efforts nearly knocked the god off the table. She expected the piece to be solid gold and therefore too heavy for her to lift. But, in fact, the statue was far lighter than she expected it to be. She abandoned the oddity in the wallpaper and stared at the statue instead. It was made of gold and painted enamel with the ruby prominent on the elephant's forehead. Sense told Caro she wouldn't be able to lift it, but when she tried all the same, she was able to raise it several inches. And as she did, something rattled in the god's belly.

"No," she gasped. "It couldn't be."

She tried to turn the statue over, looking for some kind of hinge or clasp or way to open it, but even though it was hollow, it was still heavy. She set it back on the table, ready to tip it to the side, but a mad thought struck her. Purely on instinct, she pressed the ruby in the god's forehead.

Instantly, his belly popped open and a fat diamond

that would have fit perfectly in a large soup spoon rolled out. Caro's mouth dropped open as she stared at the diamond in shock. She scooped it up, a shiver passing down her spine at how heavy and how cool the diamond was.

"Rufus."

She turned to him, but as she did, voices sounded from the room adjoining the one they were in.

"Hide," Rufus hissed, rushing toward her.

Caro had no time to do more than grab the Ganesh statue, slapping his belly shut and praying that whatever mechanism kept it closed would hold. Rufus grabbed her hand a moment later and jerked her toward one of the windows. His motion was a little too abrupt, though, and before she could think, the diamond spilled out of her hand and rolled under the table.

Rufus dragged her behind the curtain mere seconds before the door at the side of the room opened and two sets of footsteps entered the room.

"This better happen this time." Lord Hazelton's stern voice filtered through the curtain.

Caro caught her breath, every nerve in her body bristling in panic. The curtain didn't fully cover her and Rufus. A gap of about six inches flapped open immediately beside her. Through it, she could just barely make out the table, the statue of Ganesh, and the diamond, which sat in plain sight under the table, touching one of its back legs.

"The diamond is yours if you have my money," Mr.

Newman answered Lord Hazelton's statement. "Hand it over and I'll tell you where it is."

"Tell me where it is and I'll give you the money," Lord Hazelton replied.

Mr. Newman answered with a frustrated growl. "We don't have time for this. There are Bow Street Runners all through Manchester Square, and I have no doubt there are agents in the house as well."

"Then tell me where the diamond is and we can leave this place and never come back," Lord Hazelton insisted.

"Only after you give me the money," Mr. Newman said in a raised voice.

"Dammit, man," Lord Hazelton bellowed. "You told me you had a priceless diamond to sell that would be the centerpiece of my collection. Did you lie to me? Is this merely a plot to rob me of tens of thousands of pounds?"

"If I had known you would be such a shit about it, I never would have offered you the diamond in the first place," Mr. Newman snapped in return. "I risked my neck to steal that diamond. I could sell it to anyone, but I was given to understand that you were a serious collector with the blunt to purchase."

Caro slapped a hand over her mouth to stop herself from gasping at Mr. Newman's confession. He had admitted to the theft in so many words, plain as day.

As it turned out, she needn't have stopped herself from making any sort of noise. No sooner was the confession made then several loud thumps echoed in the room, followed by the sound of boots and the clicking of pistols being cocked.

"Stay right where you are," Saif Khan's voice shouted.

A moment later, Rufus pushed aside the curtain, revealing him and Caro. "I heard him," he said. "I heard Wallace Newman confess to stealing the Chandramukhi Diamond."

"I heard it as well," Caro added, stepping out from behind the curtain with him.

The contents of the room had changed drastically within a matter of seconds. The same fussy collection of furniture and decorations filled the space, but along with Rufus and Caro and Mr. Newman and Lord Hazelton, half a dozen Bow Street Runners, including Saif Khan, crowded the room.

"I didn't do anything. It wasn't me," Lord Hazelton blubbered, holding up his hands.

"We heard you confess to attempting to buy the diamond," Saif told him, a look of pure contempt in his eyes.

"You heard nothing," Mr. Newman said.

"You confessed to stealing the diamond," Caro reminded him.

Mr. Newman sneered at her. "Foolish chit. You heard playacting, that is all."

"Yes, yes," Lord Hazelton agreed, a wildness about him as he tried to keep up with what was happening. "We were rehearsing a theatrical performance, that is all."

"I don't believe it," Saif Khan said, his pistol pointed straight at Mr. Newman.

"You have to believe it, you stupid colonial," Mr. Newman said. "You have no diamond, therefore you have no theft."

Caro's glance shot to the diamond as it sat passively under the table, unnoticed by all.

"Ah, but that's where you're wrong," Saif said, marching toward Mr. Newman, pistol still raised. "I know exactly where the diamond is."

Mr. Newman shifted away from him, looking anxious. "You're lying."

"Would you like to test me on that point?" Saif said, grabbing Mr. Newman's arm even as he pressed the barrel of the pistol into the side of his head. "Would you like to test what this stupid colonial knows?"

"You don't know, you don't know anything," Mr. Newman wailed, squeezing his eyes shut and shrinking away from Saif.

"I will give you until the count of three," Saif said. "One—"

"I don't have the diamond," Mr. Newman wailed. "I swear I don't have it."

"Two—"

"It's not on me. It's hidden. I hid it. I don't have it."

Caro squeezed her eyes shut and plugged her ears with her fingers as she waited for the final, deadly "Three." But instead, Saif lowered his pistol and pushed Mr. Newman away before releasing the hammer.

"Take him away and lock him up, boys," Saif said, turning to the other Runners. "Lock both of them up."

"But you cannot prove anything," Mr. Newman insisted. "We are merely acting. You cannot prove anything."

Saif turned back to him. "You just said that you hid the diamond. It is necessary to steal a diamond before one has the ability to hide it, no?"

Mr. Newman stared at him in horror, his mouth flapping. But all too soon, he knew he'd given himself away. He burst into a sob, slumping against one of the Runners who grabbed his arms. He put up no resistance as the Runners marched him out of the room, Lord Hazelton in tow.

"That's the end of that," Saif said, walking over to shake Rufus's hand. "Thank you for your help, friend."

The relief Caro felt at the end of the caper quickly tightened into a new sort of excitement. Two Runners were still left in the room to witness what might happen next.

"It's not the end," she said. "The diamond is still missing."

"I wasn't lying when I said I knew where it was," Saif told her with an apologetic look. "I'm sorry that I couldn't give the two of you more time to find it."

He walked over to the table holding the statue of Ganesh, bowed to the god, then pressed the ruby in his forehead as Caro had. But when the statue's belly popped open, it was empty. Saif's expression dropped to alarm. "It's gone," he said, sounding genuinely surprised.

Caro nudged Rufus hard. It took Rufus a few seconds and a few more nudges to give her his attention.

"How can you give away the reward if the diamond is not found?" Caro asked, jerking her head toward the bottom of the table.

Rufus frowned at her in confusion.

"Could Newman have removed it before meeting with Hazelton?" one of the other Runners asked.

"Would your father be willing to double the reward for whoever finds the diamond?" Caro asked.

Saif glanced to her, his eyes narrowed. As he did, Caro tugged hard on Rufus's sleeve with one hand, pointing to the diamond under the table with her other hand.

"I suppose he might," Saif said, studying Caro carefully. He must have known she was up to something.

Caro tugged on Rufus's sleeve and pointed more vehemently. "It's the least he could do, should someone locate the diamond at last, considering it isn't where you thought it was."

All at once, Rufus sucked in a breath. He snapped straight, glancing to Saif with a wide grin. "Fifty thousand pounds should do the trick," he said.

"Fifty thousand pounds is highway robbery in and of itself," Saif said, laughing.

"Does your father have the money?" Rufus asked, his voice brimming with so much confidence that Caro knew he saw not only the diamond, but a way for the two of them to be together.

"Perhaps," Saif answered, a slow smile spreading across his face. "If not, my father has the ear of Emperor Akbar. The Mughal Empire would hardly miss fifty thousand pounds."

"Are you certain?" Rufus askcd. "Fifty thousand pounds would go a long way to convincing my father to allow me to marry the bride of my choice." He reached for Caro's hand, grinning at her in victory.

Saif was smiling fully as well. "Understood, my friend. I believe my father would understand as well, and he would be only too happy to give something precious in return for something precious."

"If that is the case...." Rufus let go of Caro's hand, stepped forward, and crouched so that he could reach under the table and pick up the diamond. He stood, moved to Saif, and deposited the diamond in his hand. "There you go," he said. "One priceless diamond in exchange for another." He stepped back to Caro, sliding his arm around her and winking at her.

That wasn't enough for Caro.

She let out a victorious sigh of, "We did it," and threw herself against him, lifting to her toes to bring her mouth crashing against his in a kiss that could have ignited the world.

CHAPTER 10

*T*here was surprisingly little for Caro and Rufus to do once the trap had snapped around Mr. Newman and Lord Hazelton.

"You might want to return to your school," Saif told Caro as the Runners prepared to escort Mr. Newman and Lord Hazelton out of the room. "I was told that Miss Dobson stole back into the school, thinking she would be safe there after she sensed trouble brewing."

Caro's eyes widened. "I can only imagine what Felicity and Eliza have done to her."

What, in fact, Felicity and Eliza had done to the woman was to catch her the moment she walked through the door, drag her down to the wine cellar in the school's basement, and shackle her over the barrel the same way she'd mistreated so many of her pupils in the past. As horrified as Caro was to see the older woman's backside exposed as Felicity and Eliza took turns swatting it with carpet beaters, Caro couldn't help but feel there was a certain sort of justice to the action.

"Let hor go," she said with a somewhat reluctant sigh, taking Felicity's carpet beater from her.

"Yes, let me go," Miss Dobson wailed. "I swear, I'll retire to the country, I'll move to the continent. Anything you ask of me."

"Send her to India," Eliza said, brandishing her beater threateningly.

"No, send her to New South Wales," Felicity said.

"She may go wherever she wants to go," Caro said. "Provided it is not within the British Isles. And," she quickly added, "provided she assign the ownership of this building and the school to me."

Felicity and Eliza brightened, and Miss Dobson cried out, "Anything. Anything at all. I'll have my father's solicitor draw up the transfer of ownership immediately."

Caro motioned for Felicity and Eliza to set Miss Dobson free. They did so, and the three of them escorted the vile woman up to her office.

"You realize that you may not be able to own this building or the school outright," Eliza murmured as they headed up the stairs. "The laws regarding women's ownership of property are vexing."

"It may not be a problem," Caro said, grinning at Rufus as they reached the top of the stairs. "I may simply have her transfer ownership to my husband."

Eliza's brow shot up. "Are felicitations in order?" she smiled.

"Give me tonight to sort it," Caro said with a wink.

She left Miss Dobson in the capable hands of Felicity and Eliza, as well as Rebecca and Nigel, who were ready to cart Miss Dobson off to prison as an accomplice in the theft if she failed to cooperate. That left Caro and Rufus free to leave the school and to head into the heart of Mayfair, to Herrington House.

"I still think it's madness for you to accompany me on this errand," Rufus told her as his family's confused butler let them into the house.

"Errand?" Caro shook her head incredulously. "This is a matter of life and death, and I will not be left out of it."

Rufus's father seemed to have other plans. He was already in a towering temper when he marched into the small, family parlor where Caro and Rufus had been sent to wait for him.

"What is the meaning of this?" Lord Herrington demanded as he strode into the room.

A lesser woman might have been intimidated into tears by the sight of the raging, older man, but Caro had come to do battle. "Your son is here to dictate his terms, my lord," she announced.

"Dictate his—" Lord Herrington shook his head in annoyance. "This is a matter between me and my son," he told Caro. "Please leave at once."

"Caro will stay," Rufus said, pulling himself to his full height and squaring his shoulders. "She is to be my wife."

Lord Herrington's expression darkened, and he narrowed his eyes. "We have discussed this. You will marry Lady Malvis and her fortune. What you choose to do with your affections is secondary."

"I will marry Lady Caroline," Rufus insisted, taking a step toward his father. "And I will bolster the fortunes of our family with my own fortune."

Lord Herrington blinked, confusion clear on his face. "What fortune do you refer to?"

"The reward money for recovering the Chandra-mukhi Diamond," Caro answered.

Lord Herrington glanced at her in surprise, then back to Rufus. "Explain."

"I found the diamond tonight," Rufus said, giving the barest possible explanation. "The reward for its recovery is fifty thousand pounds."

Lord Herrington looked flabbergasted. "Fifty thousand pounds?"

"Yes, Father. And I will be giving all of it to the family as a means of improving our situation."

Lord Herrington gaped at Rufus for several long moments. Caro watched his expression flicker from outrage to confusion to consideration. But all too soon, he shook his head and said, "Impossible. Fifty thousand is an immense fortune, but it is not a sustainable amount. Our landholdings need a continual infusion of income over the course of several years before they can be saved."

"Then it is imperative that your son marry a woman with a substantial income," Caro said. Her stomach filled with butterflies at the prospect of playing her trump card at last.

"Precisely," Lord Herrington said, though with a puzzled look and narrowed eyes that said he knew there was more to what she was saying. "Lady Malvis is such a woman."

"As it happens, I am also such a woman," Caro said, her grin growing.

Lord Herrington studied her. Rufus studied her with a calculating expression as well, but unlike his father, he smiled.

"Forgive me, Lady Caroline," Lord Herrington said at last, "but I am familiar with your father and your family. While his title is old and respected, his income is modest."

"I am not referring to my father's income or my dowry," Caro said, unable to keep her excitement inside. "I am referring to my own income."

"Mrs. Vickers," Rufus said with a sudden laugh. "You clever strumpet."

Lord Herrington blinked, looking both embarrassed and impressed. "Am I to understand that you are the authoress of those works of salacious fiction that are currently taking London by storm?" he asked.

"I am, my lord," Caro said with a modest nod. "And I can assure you that the income derived from such works is substantial."

"How substantial?" Lord Herrington asked. When Caro gave him the figure, both his and Rufus's jaws dropped in shock. "So much for such frivolous and scandalous works?"

"The *ton* adores frivolity and scandal, my lord," Caro said. "Though I can assure you, I will do my best to maintain the secrecy of my literary activities so as not to damage the Herrington name." Never mind that a small number of people already knew her identity. She could impress upon the Duchess of Cavendish the need for discretion. Surely the woman had enough of a heart to understand the need for secrecy.

"What do you say, Father?" Rufus asked, hope bright in his eyes. He added, "It would be quite a sensation to welcome the heroine of the recovery of the Chandramukhi Diamond into the family. I am certain Caro's part in the recovery will come to light and be celebrated."

Lord Herrington appeared impressed for a moment, but his expression quickly dropped. "Lord Cunningham will be furious when the announcement of your engagement is made."

Caro didn't care one bit about Lady Malvis. Her heart soared at the implication of Rufus's father's words. He was going to allow them to wed. They had triumphed after all.

"Thank you, Father," Rufus said, rushing forward to clasp his father in a manly hug.

"We will inform your mother of all this in the morning," Lord Herrington said, hugging Rufus in return, and looking rather relieved to Caro's eyes. "Now, take your lady love home, and we'll begin arrangements for this match in the morning."

"Yes, sir," Rufus said.

He took Caro's arm and led her out of the room. But instead of heading to the front hall and the door, Rufus glanced over his shoulder to be certain his father wasn't following them and that they weren't being observed. He veered down the hall in a different direction, whisking Caro into the servant's stairway and up.

"I'll be damned if I'm returning you to that school tonight," he whispered as they rushed up the stairs to the first floor. "You're warming my bed tonight as my betrothed, and there isn't a damned thing anyone can do to stop us."

Caro giggled, ready to wrap herself around Rufus and never let go. She had to wait as they crept as silently along the hall to his bedchamber as they could, narrowly avoiding Lord Herrington as he retired to his room as they went. Blessedly, Rufus's room was far removed from the bedrooms of his parents, and they were able to slip inside and lock the door behind them unseen.

"Thaddeus is the only one we have to worry about," he said between kisses as he backed Caro toward his bed, attempting to remove both her clothes and his as he went. "And bless him, my brother is all of nineteen. If he over-hears us, he'll be more interested in abusing himself than telling tales."

Caro laughed, "You are aware that informing me

your younger brother may eavesdrop on us is not an encouragement toward amorous activity, are you not?"

"Since when do you need encouragement toward amorous activity?" Rufus purred, undoing the ties of her gown and pulling the sleeves off her shoulders.

Caro gasped as her back pressed against one of the posts at the foot of Rufus's bed. If any other man had said such a thing to her—Lord Hazelton, for example—she would have been furiously offended. But coming from Rufus, the frank statement of her appetite sent a carnal shiver through her that centered in her sex. He peeled her bodice down to her waist and plucked at the laces of her stays.

"You are a goddess of lust," he went on, bending to shower kisses over her shoulders as he opened her stays and gathered her breasts in his hands. "You are a paragon of carnality, and I love you for it."

"Do not let my mother hear you say that," Caro laughed, then gasped as he trailed kisses across the top of her breast to close his mouth around her nipple.

She tilted her head back against the bedpost and sucked in a breath as he ignited fiery sensations within her. If she was a goddess of lust, then Rufus was a satyr and a rake who knew all too well how to elicit pleasure from a woman's body. A polite and proper woman would have been scandalized by his skill, knowing where he gained it, but she reveled in it, opening herself fully to the pleasure he imparted. It was far better to be the last and lifelong love of an experienced man than the perplexing object of a man who had no idea what a woman's body was for.

Her eyes were closed and she had just begun to sink into the beautiful warmth pulsing through her when Rufus clamped his teeth around her hardened nipple with just enough force to make her gasp.

"I've learned a few tricks from Felix," he told her with a mischievous sparkle in his eyes. "Now that we're destined to spend the rest of our lives together, I would be happy to share them all with you."

"Not as happy as I will be to learn them," she purred in return.

He made a sound of approval that sent shivers through her, then returned to work loosening her gown and pushing it down over her hips. "I want you naked and splayed in my bed," he murmured in her ear, nibbling on her earlobe as he worked for what he wanted. "I want to do things to you that Seven Dials whores would find obscene, and I want you to do those things to me as well."

"You're in luck," she answered, reaching for the buttons of his jacket as soon as he pushed her sleeves and stays off her arms, freeing her to reach for him. "I want all of those things too."

He pulled her away from the bedpost so that he could whisk her chemise up over her head, leaving her standing in front of him in nothing but her stockings. His gaze swept her body appreciatively, and he growled as though he'd like nothing more than to devour her.

But Caro had hardly begun her own games. She leaned into him, running her hands up his chest so that she could remove his jacket, and closing her mouth over his in a greedy kiss. He gripped her hips as she invaded his mouth with her tongue, then circled his hands around her bottom to lift her against his erection. He was already hard and straining against his breeches, and Caro ached to bring him out and play with him.

"Are you pleased to be marrying a wanton wife?" she asked, making quick work of his waistcoat, then tugging his shirt out of his breeches.

"More than you can know," he said in a voice rumbling with desire. He tore his shirt off over his head as Caro went to work on his breeches. "I did not relish the thought of marrying a woman who would probably blanch at the sight of a stiff cock."

"Whereas I adore such a sight," Caro said.

She proved her point by sinking to her knees and tugging Rufus's breeches down over his hips to bunch around his knees as she did so. He let out a sharp sound of pleasure as his cock leapt free of its confinement and stood straight up. That sound turned to a long, deep groan of pleasure as Caro took hold of him, treating him to a few, quick strokes, then leaned in to draw his head into her mouth.

It had been so long since she'd been able to put the skills she'd learned that fateful summer to good use, but every nuance of pleasure that her one other lover had instilled in her came rushing back to her. She teased

Rufus's tip with her tongue, causing him to gasp and the muscles of his groin to clench in response. She then drew him in slowly, teasingly, making him wonder just how far she was capable of going. All the while, she used her tongue and gently-applied pressure to treat every inch of him to sensation.

"You're going to be the death of me, Caro," he gasped as she drew him in so far she was in danger of choking. He reached for the bedpost, balancing himself against it as his hips twitched involuntarily.

Mischief raced through her. She held his thighs tightly and moved against him, wondering how far she could push him. He'd exhibited amazing control that first time, in her room at the school, and while she had never truly enjoyed the sensation of a man spilling himself in her mouth, she wanted to drive Rufus right to the edge of doing exactly that. So she moved fast and hard, so much so that her eyes watered.

Rufus swore and grasped a handful of her hair. "I'd marry you even if my father forbid it," he gasped.

Within seconds, he'd reached the end of his control. He wrenched away from her, panting, sweat slicking his face and chest. He only paused for a moment to catch his breath before bending to lift her off her feet, practically tossing her onto his bed. Caro gasped and wriggled as he crawled onto the bed after her, grabbing her knees and thrusting them apart with fierce command.

"Such a naughty woman," he growled, then lowered himself to lightly bite the inside of one of her thighs.

The unexpectedness of the move caused her to suck in a breath. He stretched her open even wider, holding her legs too firmly for her to move. She writhed all the same, excited by the touch of helplessness she felt. When he brought his hungry mouth to the slit of her sex, then parted her lip with his hands so that he could lick and tease her, she cried out and gripped the bedsheets desperately.

It was his turn to tease her with pleasure until she was ready to burst. He knew just how to stroke and thrust in a way that claimed ownership of her while giving so much pleasure in return. He was a master in the art of sensuality, circling her clitoris with his tongue until she was nearly weeping with desire. She deliberately held out as long as she could, wanting the pleasure to build to towering heights and to last as long as possible.

She was so close that her body buzzed with imminent release when he pulled back and whispered the single word, "Stubborn."

For a moment, she was suspended in a cloud of near orgasm. Before she could beg him to finish her, though, he reached for her and flipped her to her stomach. She barely had time to get her bearings before he lifted her hips and crashed into her.

The suddenness of his thrust and the glorious way he stretched and filled her shot her straight back to the edge of orgasm. He pounded into her with strength and depth that left her in no question of his power and his adoration. She cried and moaned in time to his thrusts and the carnal sounds he made. The sensation of her breasts jerking freely as he mated with her only added to the overall sensation of being thoroughly and deliciously fucked.

She came so hard that it nearly brought tears to her eyes. Her whole body reverberated with the contractions that milked him as he thrust. His sounds grew victorious as she gave herself completely to mating with him, rocking with him as she squeezed him. All at once, his sounds grew pitched, and his body clenched around her as he spilled his seed inside her. The moment was so perfect that Caro laughed and cried together.

The last thing she wanted was for the passion to fade, but the deep, warm sense of their souls intertwined followed the ebbing of lust. They collapsed to the bed, crawling under the covers, then seeking out each other's arms. He kissed her, not as a prelude to lovemaking, but as a lingering promise. They were so much more to each other than bedmates, and they always would be.

"I truly do love you, you know," Rufus said as he worked to catch his breath. "Not just because your appetites match my own."

"I know," Caro said. "Because I love you just as much. You're witty and determined. You're strong, but also kind. And I am convinced that you would have found a way to restore your family to its rightful place even without me or marriage or diamonds."

"No," he said, brushing damp hair back from her face. "I never could have done any of this without you." She wanted to argue with him, but he went on with, "We are a team, you and I. Without you, I was merely a suspect in a crime. With you, I can do anything."

Caro grinned, her heart so full it was near bursting. "Well, then. We'll simply have to stay together forever, won't we?"

"Forever," he said, then stole another kiss that could have ignited the ocean.

EPILOGUE

hristmas at the school formerly known as Miss Dobson's Finishing School was a delightfully merry occasion. While some of the young ladies had chosen to return to the bosom of their family for the holidays, a surprising number decided to stay.

"My parents are passing the season in Italy," Eliza declared as she stole a spoonful of Felicity's pudding. "And they're welcome to it."

"I wouldn't mind spending the holidays in Italy," Ophelia said with a sigh, glancing out the frost-covered window as though it looked out on a Tuscan vista. "It's certainly better than freezing London."

"London isn't so bad," Felicity said, striking Eliza's spoon with hers as she attempted to steal a second bit of pudding. The result was a short but exciting spoon sword-fight. "Although I wouldn't turn down a holiday somewhere light and sunny. Even a country house.

Surely, we all must have country estates in sunnier climes that we can visit."

All at once, Eliza sat straight. "You know who now has a charming country house?" she asked. When Felicity and Ophelia merely looked at her in question, she went on with, "Why, our dear Caro." A smile spread across her face. "Lady Caroline Herrington is now the proud possessor of a simply charming estate in Shropshire. My parents are on good terms with Lord Herrington the elder, and we were all invited to a house party there three years ago."

"A house party," Ophelia said with a dreamy sigh. "I have always wanted to be asked to a house party."

"House parties are divine," Felicity agreed. "Nothing is livelier than a house filled with men and women searching for mates."

"Particularly when a good portion of those men and women creep through the halls at night, in search of trouble of a particular kind," Eliza added with a wink.

Ophelia, who may or may not have been paying full attention, sat straighter. "We could all find husbands at a house party. I know we could."

"Husbands, yes," Felicity said, sharing a wicked grin with Eliza. "That's what we could find."

"Do you suppose Lady Caroline would consent to hosting a house party this summer?" Ophelia asked.

Eliza and Felicity instantly brightened.

"That would be perfect," Eliza said. "And I'm sure if we explained things, she would be all too happy to host one. After all—" she turned to Felicity, "—our prospects for freedom would be much greater if we were married and out of the influence of our families."

"Our absentee, unfeeling families," Felicity agreed with a sigh. There was a somewhat depressed pause before she went on with, "It's settled, then. We implore Caro to host a house party this summer and to invite the three of us—and whichever other young ladies she deems worthy—along with as many eligible, young friends of Lord Herrington and Lord Lichfield who she can extend invitations to."

"That would be wonderful," Ophelia said, the spark in her eyes more innocent than that lighting the other two's expressions.

"It's bound to be a grand time," Eliza agreed. "Who knows what might happen to us all?"

I HOPE YOU'VE ENJOYED CARO AND RUFUS'S STORY! At last, the Chandramukhi Diamond has been found! But if you think that's the end of the stories of the Wicked Wallflowers, well, then you don't know me well enough yet. Rufus wasn't lying when he told Caro that the chances of the young ladies left at Miss Dobson's school finding respectable mates and being accepted by the *ton* was slim. Which is why they will have to take things into their own hands. But I think we all know Miss Felicity Murdoch and Lady Eliza Towers are up to the challenge. And they have plans for their good friend, Lady Ophelia, as well! So keep your eyes peeled later this summer for the next three books in the *When the Wall-flowers were Wicked* series!

IF YOU ENJOYED THIS BOOK AND WOULD LIKE TO HEAR more from me, please sign up for my newsletter! When you sign up, you'll get a free, full-length novella, *A Passionate Deception*. Victorian identity theft has never been so exciting in this story of hope, tricks, and starting over. Part of my *West Meets East* series, *A Passionate Deception* can be read as a stand-alone. Pick up your free copy today by signing up to receive my newsletter (which I only send out when I have a new release)!

SIGN UP HERE: HTTP://EEPURL.COM/CBAVMH

Click here for a complete list of other works by Merry Farmer.

ABOUT THE AUTHOR

I hope you have enjoyed *The Clever Strumpet.* If you'd like to be the first to learn about when new books in the series come out and more, please sign up for my newsletter here: http://eepurl.com/cbaVMH And remember, Read it, Review it, Share it! For a complete list of works by Merry Farmer with links, please visit http://wp.me/P5ttjb-14F.

Merry Farmer is an award-winning novelist who lives in suburban Philadelphia with her cats, Torpedo, her grumpy old man, and Justine, her hyperactive new baby. She has been writing since she was ten years old and realized one day that she didn't have to wait for the teacher to assign a creative writing project to write something. It was the best day of her life. She then went on to earn not one but two degrees in History so that she would always have something to write about. Her books have reached the Top 100 at Amazon, iBooks, and Barnes & Noble, and have been named finalists in the prestigious RONE and Rom Com Reader's Crown awards.

ACKNOWLEDGMENTS

I owe a huge debt of gratitude to my awesome beta-readers, Caroline Lee and Jolene Stewart, for their suggestions and advice. And double thanks to Julie Tague, for being a truly excellent editor and assistant! Thanks also to the members of the Historical Harlots Facebook Group, who provide me with all sorts of inspiration!

Click here for a complete list of other works by Merry Farmer.

Made in the USA
Las Vegas, NV
01 November 2021

33499638R00095